THE LATE HOUR

STORIES FOR THE INSOMNIAC

Volume II

THE LATE HOUR

STORIES FOR THE INSOMNIAC

Volume II

Chris DelSalvo
Story Editor: Dina Diaz

Dedicated to the restless...

Contents

One Way Love

The second week of the new year unleashed the mother of all hurricanes upon California. Hurricane Veronica. She started innocently enough as a puny two-day storm off the coast of Ensenada, Mexico. But lo and behold, climate change had other plans. That unassuming tropical thunderstorm morphed into a full-blown freak cyclone, catching the unsuspecting populace off-guard. In a matter of days, coastal towns were obliterated by Veronica's relentless waves, which were frothing like the mouth of a rabid dog with a bark that meant business. She heartlessly demolished harbored boats as if they were mere playthings. She showed no mercy. The roads, freeways, and byways turned into a chaotic mess of bumper-to-bumper traffic. If Veronica was in town, forget about keeping appointments—nobody stood a chance. Not a soul. Hurricane Veronica had Southern California wrapped around her tempestuous finger. But among all the property damage and lost time, one sixteen-year-old boy felt the storm's weight on a whole other level.

Devell Lewis, or Dev as he was known to his nearest and dearest, lay sprawled on his bed, rocking a trusty gray hoodie that he wore rain or shine. At his feet stood a plastic hamper filled with warm, freshly dried clothes, a gesture to appease his Mom. Dev knew all too well that a grumpy mother before bedtime could turn into a restless parent through the night. Although he didn't often find himself in hot water, Dev had a knack for catching up in the occasional teenage drama. Nothing major, just your run-of-the-mill angst-fueled mishaps. His most recent blunder involved forgetting to return the milk to the fridge after pouring himself a bowl of cereal. Upon returning from an okay day at work, his Mom walked through the door, ready to unwind—until she spotted the milk left on the counter. Her mood quickly shifted to frustration as she realized nearly a gallon had gone to waste. With today's prices, that was a tragedy of epic suburban proportions.

Dev found himself grounded for an entire weekend as punishment but took it in stride. No cell phone or wild adventures were needed to keep him entertained. He dove into a pile of neglected skater magazines. Dev read them all, determined to make the most of his confinement. However, this time was different. Dev couldn't afford to stir up trouble with Mom and Dad. He had to be on his absolute best behavior without raising suspicion if he wanted to slip out later in the stormy night. It was a delicate dance of conveniently forgetting to say "thank you" when his Mom handed him his dinner plate. The menu that evening? Baked salmon and roasted red potatoes. It was his least favorite meal.

After dinner and some casual chitchat, Dev volunteered to do the dishes to make up for his dinner etiquette blunder. Dev went above and beyond to avoid any situation jeopardizing his chance to see Valerie. Regardless of how meticulously he had planned, Dev had no power over Hurricane Veronica. She was uncontrollable.

Lying on his back, Dev gazed up at the ceiling, intently listening to the rain pelting against the shingles of his humble single-story abode. The realization of having to venture out in the hurricane finally settled in the pit of his stomach, casting a heavy veil of melancholy over him. Would he brave the slick, wet streets on his skateboard to be with his beloved Valerie?

The logical part of his brain suggested postponing their night together. However, he was uncertain when both of Valerie's parents would be gone from the house. Valerie's mother had flown off to visit her family in Mexico, while her father, generally assigned to the morning shift as a truck driver, had swapped schedules with the evening driver because of a family emergency. Their window of romance was delicately timed, with the stars seemingly aligning. Except...

Veronica rattled the windows with her heavy winds as if mocking Dev's plans.

Dev blinked, momentarily snapping out of his deep thoughts. He turned his gaze towards the window. Dev silently watched droplets of rainwater, a dramatic symbol of the tears he wanted to shed, trickle down the plate glass frame. Suddenly, his cell phone buzzed at his side, jolting him from introspection.

With a cold and clammy hand, Dev fished out his phone from the cozy pocket of his sweater, unlocking the screen with an eager swipe. After his eyes adjusted to the brightness of the screen, Dev read:

11:30 PM

VAL

My Dad left for work.

A pause. Dev's heart raced. Another message appeared.

11:31 PM

VAL

The rain isn't letting up. Cancel?

The thunder bellowed, shaking the very core of the atmosphere. Dev's heart continued to rumble in his chest as the thunder faded. He placed his cell phone face-down on his slender torso, lost in contemplation. Thoughts swirled through his mind like the wind outside. Should he cancel their plans for the night? Valerie was a sensible girl. She would understand. But deep down, he knew that she longed for his touch just as fervently as he yearned for hers.

But the rain?

Veronica unleashed a fierce breath. She exhaled a powerful gust of wind that whipped the branches of an overgrown bush, causing them to scrape ominously against Dev's bedroom window. In a moment of rebelliousness, he bounded to the edge of his bed. Rational thought, no matter how sound, was no match for the intimate touch of a naked hand.

Fuck the rain.

Dev feverishly typed on his phone:

11:35 PM

DEV

Address?

He hit the send button, firing off the message to his girlfriend. She lived in a notorious neighborhood infamous for its relentless gang violence. A neighborhood everyone in their city called "The One Ways."

To an outsider, the five-block neighborhood comprised a twisted maze of narrow, one-way streets. Dev knew all too well the dangers that lurked within those unforgiving roads. It wasn't just about the tangled web of asphalt. It was the ominous presence of the gang that held sway over those streets. In the eyes of Cinco Puntos, the gang that watched over the poverty-stricken neighborhood, Dev was a target. As a young black male, they despised his existence and would stop at nothing to unleash their brutality upon any interloper of color.

Dev's heart raced, acutely aware of the risks he faced. Yet, stubborn love compelled him to take the risk. Her reply flashed on the screen.

11:36 PM

VAL

Are you serious? Dev!

11:36 PM

DEV

Don't worry. I'll be good. Address?

11:37 PM

VAL

DEV!

11:37 PM

DEV

I'll cut through the neighborhoods. The trees will block the rain.

Dev's eyes remained fixated on the screen, a spectator to the mesmerizing dance of pulsating text bubbles. They appeared, then disappeared, teasing him with their unpredictable rhythm. It felt like an eternity, stretching that fleeting minute into an endless expanse. The weight of anticipation bore heavily upon his shoulders, tinged with nerves and excitement. He sensed her apprehension. A fluttering uncertainty mirrored his own, yet he remained clueless about the words that would soon grace his screen. And then, at long last, her response materialized like a precious gem gleaming in the digital abyss.

11:38 PM

VAL

661 ½ Cheshire St. See you soon. BE CAREFUL.

Relieved, excited, and plagued by a twinge of fear, Dev let out a sigh that carried the weight of anticipation. After firing off his reply, a sudden wave of insecurity crashed over him. As a keen skater, his legs possessed strength and power, but the rest of his physique lacked the chiseled definition that society seemed to admire. Despite others seeing him as lean and fit, Dev's perception painted a picture of scrawniness and undesirability. When the pivotal moment arrived, would she be turned off by his body? Would she mock his very being? The thought of facing rejection from the girl he had asked to the winter formal just a year ago haunted his mind.

It was a memorable night, that winter formal. When the dance had concluded, they found themselves at a local burger joint, enjoying a large plate of chili cheese fries. Immersed in the tantalizing aroma and the molten cheese that begged for indulgence, Dev summoned every ounce of courage. While his eyes never parted from the melted cheese as he picked at it, his words stumbled and faltered. In the end, he conveyed his heartfelt message, albeit clumsily. "I... I don't know. We should be together. I think we are, uh... a good couple. Right?"

Dev looked up at her, his cheeks flushed a shade of crimson. It was a rare sight for Valerie, who usually saw him as the epitome of confidence, mainly when he showcased his latest skate trick to impress her. But in that vulnerable moment, with the food nestled between them, she found his insecurities even more endearing.

A playful smile graced Valerie's lips as she brushed back a strand of her hair. Armed with a fork, she deftly pierced a crispy golden fry coated in a delectable layer of chili cheese goodness. With a gentle touch, she brought it to Dev's lips, feeding him the tempting morsel. "I think we're good together, too." Her voice was filled with affirmation and tenderness.

A long strand of cheese dangled from Dev's mouth, but he couldn't help but smile. From that moment on, they had become inseparable. Their journey as a couple had been filled with laughter, shared experiences, and the warmth of their connection.

As his mind wandered, the weight of the decision to see his girl in the roughest part of town—during a storm—anchored him back to the present. Dev sank into his bed, lost in thought. Doubt consumed him. But his cell phone vibrated just as he was on the verge of uncertainty. Dev looked at his phone, and the message read:

11:39 PM
VAL
I love you.

Valerie's message was the jolt of motivation he needed to get his ass into gear. Dev swiftly placed his phone aside and grabbed his shoes. The relentless rain outside had intensified, now cascading down upon the world with a ferocity that resembled a barrage of bullets hitting the roof. Undeterred by the torrential downpour, Dev tied his shoes with determination. He was prepared to brave the elements, traverse the soaked streets, and navigate the treacherous maze of The One Ways. No obstacle would stand in his way. For love, he was ready to face whatever challenges lay ahead.

A sense of stillness and darkness enveloped the homes on a peculiar J-shaped block of Longworth Avenue. The chilly winds and rhythmic raindrops made it seem as if the entire neighborhood was asleep. The only sign of life was the bluish glow of a flickering television in one of the living rooms. Suddenly, a bolt of lightning whipped across the swollen clouds. A low thunder soon followed.

Dev's older brother, Robert, sat on a worn brown couch, clad in a thermal shirt and faded sweatpants. With the freedom of youth and the absence of academic burdens, Robert relished staying up late, immersing himself in slasher movies—a guilty pleasure he had been deprived of until recently. As a mediocre student, he had grown weary of the education system dictating his every move, from what to study to how to dress and even what to think. Thus, when graduation finally set him free last June, he had no intention of returning to the academic saddle.

Despite their parents' concern for their eldest son's future, they reluctantly agreed, with a few conditions, to Robert's year-long break from school. One of those conditions was that he had to maintain the house. This entailed daily chores such as taking out the trash, sweeping the floors, and cleaning both restrooms, all to be completed before their parents returned from work. If an institution had granted a prize for the best-kept house in the neighborhood, Robert Lewis would have undoubtedly claimed the top spot. He breezed through the tasks effortlessly.

The last condition, and one from which he couldn't escape, was that he had to find a part-time job. True to his promise, Robert secured a job at the local movie theater a few weeks after his graduation. Working only a few hours in the evenings granted him the freedom he yearned for. He reveled in his ample time to himself, but the opportunity to rub it in his brother's face every chance he got brought him the most satisfaction. Sibling rivalry and tough love—they were an inseparable duo.

Despite the pouring rain, Robert's ears perked up as he heard the faint creak of Dev's bedroom door opening from the darkened hallway. He loved his little brother, but he also enjoyed teasing him. After all, what are big brothers for if not to give their siblings a hard time? The anticipation grew as Robert pretended to watch the cliché horror movie, its only saving grace being the hot blonde on screen. He patiently waited for Dev to unwittingly step on the loose floorboards their father had never gotten around to fixing. But as the seconds ticked by and the expected creak never came, Robert knew that Dev was up to something mischievous. That realization brought a grin to Robert's face.

Oh, this is going to be fun, he thought.

"Isn't it past your bedtime?" Robert taunted as he reached for a bag of white chocolate-covered pretzels on the coffee table.

"Shut up," Dev muttered, his grip on his skateboard tightening.

Savoring his role as the older brother, Robert reclined on the couch, devouring his snack with an air of superiority. Propping his feet up on the coffee table, he continued in a self-assured tone, "What? Speak up. The rain is making it—"

"Ssh!" Dev interjected, moving closer to Robert to silence him. In haste, he inadvertently stepped on the loose floorboards he had been avoiding. The resulting creak echoed through the room, causing Dev to cringe. Rather than focusing on the empty calories he was consuming, Robert found greater pleasure in what was unfolding.

With a playful glint in his eyes, he asked, "What are you up to?"

"I'm going out."

"On a school night?"

"Yeah. And?"

"But it's pouring."

"No, shit."

"Do Mom and Dad know?" He knew the answer but wanted to hear what Dev would say.

Robert's ears perked up as he heard a familiar sound—roller wheels shifting behind him. Intrigued, he stood up and quizzically asked, "Seriously, dude? Where are you off to?" He turned around and spotted Dev in his gray hoodie, gripping his skateboard tightly.

Knowing there was no point in lying and needing to leave immediately, Dev responded, "I'm going to see Valerie." He pulled the hoodie over his head and adjusted his posture, displaying his conviction to Robert. "And if you tell Mom and Dad, we're going to have a problem, alright?"

Robert couldn't help but smirk. He knew he deserved that threat for teasing Dev, and deep down, he admired his brother's determination to brave the elements to be with his girlfriend. How could he possibly deny him that adventure?

Softening his tone, Robert asked, "How far are you going?"

Dev evaded the question, aware of the reaction it would trigger. Swallowing hard, he whispered through the static sound of rain, "The One Ways."

At that moment, the wind howled as if the words that escaped Dev's lips had invoked Veronica herself. This caused her to stir restlessly through the trees and shrubs, unleashing a mighty gasp of fear and astonishment.

Robert's face dropped. "The One Ways!"

"Come on, dude, shut up," Dev snapped back, glancing towards his parents' darkened room down the hallway. He couldn't hear any signs of them stirring.

Robert lunged towards his brother, clumsily maneuvering around the edge of the couch and hitting his shin on the corner. Ignoring the throbbing pain, he desperately exclaimed, "Are you out of your mind?" He grabbed Dev's shoulder firmly, holding him in place before he could reach for the door.

"You can't go to the One Ways," Robert pleaded, locking eyes with his brother. The insanity reflected in Dev's gaze sent shivers down his spine. In the fleeting silence surrounding them, Robert relived a brief period when their family resided in a modest two-bedroom starter home on Hopland Avenue.

Unbeknownst to their naive parents at the time, the house was perilously close to the destructive force of gang violence that lurked just down a narrow stretch of residential roads. The housing and parking were crammed together, leaving no room for comfort, as if every inch of available real estate had been sparingly used in the suffocating development.

Robert's encounter with a prowler near the One Ways during a sleepless night flashed back to him. It was an event that shaped his fear of the dark—the night had begun with the cacophony of barking neighborhood dogs. However, it failed to rouse his deeply sleeping parents, who remained blissfully unaware in the adjacent room. Coincidentally, the swift tapping on Robert's bedroom window snapped him awake from near slumber.

Tap, tap, tap!

The rapid succession of tapping, coupled with the enigmatic terrors of the night, seized hold of Robert's imagination. He clutched the blue sheet tightly, yearning for the comforting presence of his parents, but found only an empty room devoid of solace. He waited, hoping the tapping would cease.

Tap, tap, tap!

It beckoned him to pull open the shades, whatever lurked outside. Trembling beneath his sheets, Robert prayed that by waiting it out, the torment would...

TAP! TAP! TAP!

Robert longed to leap out of bed, burst through his parents' bedroom door, and scream at the top of his lungs about the relentless tapping outside his window. But he would have to traverse the pitch-dark hallway to reach them, which was out of the question. It was easier for his frayed nerves to face the mystery alone than to venture into the unknown depths of the carpeted hallway. Sliding off the bed, he mustered the courage to approach the window, drawn to the ceaseless tapping. His hands grasped the edges of the puppy-patterned shades, squirming in his baggy pajamas as he pulled them open.

Robert squinted his eyes and jerked the curtains apart, only to be met with darkness. A sigh of relief escaped him as his racing pulse began to calm. But then, his heart sank as he noticed the abyss shifting towards him, like unruly waves that refused to find peace. The abyss—the darkness—revealed itself as the black hooded jacket of a desperate man seeking refuge. Robert locked eyes with the man's haunting gaze, his hands resting on the windowsill as if he were a timid soul begging for redemption in the sanctuary of a church pew.

"Let me in," he pleaded, his voice filled with desperation, reaching out to a terrified Robert.

Robert couldn't find his voice. The gravity of the situation, which called for an adult's intervention, rendered him speechless and immobile.

"Open the window. Let... me... IN!"

His frantic words were punctuated by the uproar of barking dogs growing closer from the neighboring property. Someone was rapidly approaching, driven by an unknown purpose. The trepidation etched on the stranger's face spoke volumes about his desperate situation. Even at the tender age of five, Robert understood that his only hope lay in granting the man entry.

Frustrated by Robert's hesitant gaze, the disheveled man in the black hoodie glanced over his shoulder, sensing the imminent danger closing in. With a swift motion, he snapped his attention back to the bewildered boy while the neighborhood dogs behind him grew more ferocious and relentless in their barking.

Losing his patience, he demanded, "Let me in!"

Startled by his sudden outburst, Robert snapped out of his daze, his nerves spiraling out of control. He shook his head vigorously, like a malfunctioning toy caught in an endless loop, until the troubled stranger grew tired of his wavering hesitation.

"You *fuckin'* nigger!" The drifter unleashed a powerful punch, shattering the plate glass window with a frustrated blow. Recoiling from the windowsill, his black cowlick falling over his eyes, he sprang to his feet. Robert had sealed his fate. The man's snarl, distorted by fractured glass shards, etched his savage image into Robert's memory forever.

Catatonic, Robert watched through the broken bedroom window as the stranger bolted for the front yard while two imposing silhouettes jumped over the brick wall. These tattooed thugs, their faces concealed in the darkness of the night, landed on a budding strawberry bush that Robert's mother had recently planted. Beneath their rubber soles, they crushed her precious fruits, staining them a sinister shade of red. Their legs propelled them over the makeshift garden, racing across the yard. In their relentless pursuit of the drifter, Robert caught a glimpse of their pocket knives, their steel blades gleaming under the orange glow of a nearby streetlamp. The reflection of their daggers, multiplied by the shattered glass, stirred more emotions within Robert than the savage snarl of the stranger, urging him to unleash a long-withheld cry for help.

His piercing and raw screams, echoing through the night fourteen years ago, not only summoned his parents to his room, prompting their hasty relocation to Longworth Avenue, but also brought him back to the present.

In the living room, driven by his desires, his teenage brother hovered on the edge of returning to their old neighborhood—the infamous "One Ways."

"Dev..." Robert's words trailed off as the memory of that unfortunate night faded away.

Dev shrugged off Robert's hand on his shoulder, readjusting the weight of his skateboard, and assertively declared, "Hold your breath. It's already done." Robert's train of thought, reignited by his brother's unwavering resolve to pursue his romantic escapade, gave way to a stern reprimand that would make their parents proud.

"What will happen if someone catches you sneaking into her room? Huh? They'll drag you out into the middle of the street and kill you. And you know why? Because you're black."

Dev met Robert's gaze, his eyes glossy, and stated, "It's getting late. I've gotta go."

"Jesus Christ, Dev..." Robert paused. His mind flooded with the hushed warnings he had heard all his life within their close-knit community. "You don't mess with the One Ways."

Dev sighed, admitting, "I know."

Amplified by the unyielding rain, their silence trapped them in a deadlock.

"I can't let you go," Robert declared.

"Then wake up Mom and Dad," Dev retorted, the wheels of his skateboard gently swaying as he positioned himself near the door. "I'm outta here."

Robert reached out with a hand that could not hold him back. Desperation laced his voice as he pleaded, "Can't you wait until the rain dies down?"

Ignoring his brother's plea, Dev turned his back and carefully unlocked the door. As he opened it, the scent of wet pavement filled their nostrils. The rain's melody, Veronica's symphony, soothing to many, terrified Robert to his core.

"Wait," Robert exclaimed in a final attempt to save his brother from venturing into the cold, wet streets.

At the threshold, Dev halted. Akin to a cowboy stepping out of a saloon, he looked over his shoulder and asked, "What?"

"Text me once you've reached her place. If you don't, I'll wake up Mom and Dad. I'll tell them where you went."

It was a reasonable compromise. Dev turned around, noticing the sincerity in his brother's demeanor. He nodded and prepared to leave, but

Robert held him back once again.

"Hold on."

"This is getting old, dude."

Brushing off the comment, Robert assessed his brother from head to toe. "You'll be soaked as soon as you reach the end of the block." He went to the kitchen and said, "Follow me."

"What for?"

"Don't be a dick. It'll only take a second." Robert left him behind, confident that his brother wouldn't abandon him. And true to his expectation, Robert was right.

Dev closed the door and trailed after Robert, skateboard in hand, into the kitchen. Robert switched on the light and moved towards the sink. He knelt and opened the bottom drawers.

Dev, dumbfounded, observed as Robert rummaged through the assortment of canned goods and cleaning supplies they had hoarded over the years.

"You're making too much noise," Dev whispered.

"Shut up," Robert retorted.

Robert's search came to an end. Beneath a bucket of partially used plaster, he discovered a carton of heavy-duty trash bags their father had purchased in preparation for their grandmother's eightieth birthday party. Mindful of the noise, Robert carefully retrieved the box of trash bags and brought it to the countertop.

"What are you doing?" Dev asked.

"Saving your ass."

Robert unrolled a blue trash bag and handed it to his agitated brother. "Put your board down," Robert instructed. He reached for the kitchen cutlery before him and extracted a pair of shears from its wooden cradle.

"I need you to stretch that out like a shirt. Fold the bottom part up."

All Dev wanted was to leave, so he complied with his brother's demands without further protest. Before proceeding, Dev leaned his skateboard against a bottom cabinet drawer, carefully positioning the wheels to face away from the polished surface. He knew that if he didn't secure his skateboard correctly, the wheels would roll off and potentially wake their parents. With his skateboard securely positioned, Dev stretched the trash bag in front of Robert as he approached with the shears.

"Hold it tight," Robert ordered.

Using the sharp tip of the shears, Robert pierced the center seam of the bag, creating a clean, one-foot-long slit. He then turned to his younger brother and instructed, "Get inside the bag, like a...""I see what you're doing," Dev interrupted with a smile. "Okay."

In less than five minutes, Robert set up his brother in the makeshift poncho. Aside from learning how to take a crap out on the great outdoors, it was the only helpful skill he had learned during his brief time with the Boy Scouts.

Dev sported two trash bags, using the first to shield his sweatshirt and the second as an extra layer of protection, complete with a makeshift torn-out hoodie. The plastic poncho was cleverly cut on both sides to accommodate his arms, though it felt a tad snug around his shoulders. Nonetheless, the poncho fitted well, and Dev couldn't help but admire his reflection in the window above the sink. He gave himself a once-over with a faint smirk, thoroughly pleased with his new fit.

"How does it feel?"

Turning away from his reflection, Dev slipped the blue plastic hoodie over his head, his excitement evident. "Dude, this is awesome. Thanks."

Robert stuffed his hands in his pockets and reminded him firmly, "Text me when you get to her place." He added, pausing for emphasis, "And... when you're coming back home."

"That wasn't part of the deal."

"That's because this isn't a negotiation."

Dev scoffed, "Okay, Mom."

Robert smirked. "Be careful out there."

Just as Dev was about to argue that their town was far from the eye of the storm, a thunderous wind swept across the neighborhood, instantly silencing him. The house trembled beneath their feet, and with sunken gazes, they turned away from each other to look out the window.

~

Stretched against the stormy skyline, trees swayed to the forceful winds in a rhythmic dance. Dampened leaves broke free from their bare branches and floated through the air, scattering across the quiet neighborhood where parked cars and still houses lined an extended, rain-soaked road. The gentle downpour had brought a rare tranquility to the town, suspending the worries and troubles of the outside world. Even the most restless sleepers had traded the glow of their televisions for the warm embrace of their beds.

Suddenly, an old, battered car emerged from a distant block. Its aged engine coughed and sputtered, shattering the calm night. Dim headlights struggled to pierce the darkness, guiding the vehicle to a stop. The car, a blend of gray and charcoal, pulled up beside a storm drain choked with foliage and litter, turning the gutter into a murky pool of water.

Hidden in the shadows, the driver waited momentarily at the stop sign as the car's outdated windshield wipers could not keep pace with the pouring rain. Growing impatient, the driver shifted the manual transmission into first gear, causing the hood to rattle as the cogs engaged. The worn-out tires plunged into the flooded gutter, and as the car emerged from the puddle, a streak of blue whizzed right past the driver.

Oblivious to the looming heap of scrap metal because of its dim headlights, and with the 90's R&B tune "Every Little Thing You Do" blaring in his headphones, muffled by the gusty wind, Dev narrowly avoided the vehicle as it neared the stop sign. Its warning signals went unnoticed in his brief lapse of attention.

With the beat-up car's broken tail lights and its horn fading into the distance, Dev maintained his stance on the skateboard beneath his Vans. The adrenaline rush from the near miss and the infectious chorus playing in his headphones sharpened his focus. Usually, he relied on the sidewalks to navigate his way, but Veronica's wild winds had littered the path in front of his house, forcing him to adapt.

Luckily, the two-seater that had nearly collided with him was the last car he encountered on his journey toward the bustling intersection of Firestone and Imperial Highway. Thanks to the makeshift poncho crafted by Robert, his torso remained dry despite the downpour. His pants and eyesight were another story. Still, he pushed his back foot forward, gliding along the slippery road while using the back of his hand to wipe raindrops from his eyes.

Dev's skateboard hurtled toward a fork in the road at breakneck speed. With no hint of impulse, he veered left. Every movement of his board, every shift in his weight, and every kick he made had been meticulously planned before he stepped out of his bedroom. As a minor, he knew the curfew-enforcing deputies and sheriffs could set back his freedom by a few years. Growing up in Norwalk, Dev was aware of their constant presence, patrolling the streets in their black and white cars, armed with citation slips and handcuffs. If he wanted to evade their watchful patrol, he needed a foolproof plan. Or at least, that was what he believed.

Dev skidded his back foot on the slick asphalt, teetering on the edge of losing his balance between a Jack In The Box and a closed pizza parlor. As he neared the intersection of Firestone Boulevard and Imperial Highway, he leaped off his skateboard, stomping the tail forcefully and snatching it up. The wide-open intersection exposed him, susceptible to the scrutiny of passing cops and nosy onlookers keen to meddle in others' affairs. Much like the adjacent 24-hour drive-thru, the expansive road lay deserted, without any vehicles.

Taking a deep breath, he exhaled a visible vapor cloud and sprinted across the street, seizing the moment. His love song for the night faded from his ears, allowing him to hear the dull rain rattling against his plastic hoodie. His footsteps echoed as he ran past a narrow center divider. He then cut through a deserted gas station. Its vivid neon sign projected a dreamy red and blue glow onto the tranquil road.

Suddenly, an air horn blared through the wild air, assaulting his ears. Wide-eyed, Dev spotted a railroad crossing separating a residential neighborhood from a car dealership and a private Christian school. The crossing's red flashing lights provided an extra boost to his already lightning-fast feet. His elongated shadow stretched behind him as the barrier arms of the railroad crossing began their descent. The clunky sound of his skateboard and the warning horn of the approaching train gradually faded into the background, drowned out by the melodic strings of a song.

He spotted the train's glaring lights rapidly approaching from the side. Thankfully, there was still enough distance between him and the train to safely cross without risking a close encounter. The barrier arms locked into place, and with a swift crouch, Dev slipped under them, making sure his shoes didn't get trapped between the steel gaps of the railroad.

Breathless and chilled to the bone but determined, he tossed his skateboard onto the road. He hopped onto the black grip tape and propelled himself forward with a forceful kick from his back foot. Before he knew it, he entered a neighborhood like his home street. With the music pulsing in his ears, the train passed through the railroad crossing behind him, rattling nearby homes. Despite the rumbling boxcars, tonight, no one woke up.

Navigating through the familiar streets of Norwalk, Dev took a sharp left at a two-way split. Racing down the middle of Ratliffe Street, he gazed up and caught sight of the towering fluorescent lights of a community park drawing nearer. It was Vista Verde. Much like the deluge inundating the city, the memories of the park flooded his memory.

He reminisced about a not-too-distant spring break when he had skateboarded in that park and unexpectedly encountered Valerie and her classmates taking pictures for their photography class. After Dev and Valerie's final exams in Mrs. Lettermen's algebra class, their budding relationship had abruptly come to an end. When they were assigned to different homerooms, it was challenging for him to adjust to the second half of the school year. He missed making her laugh before class, something his new history seatmate didn't much appreciate. Since then, Dev had only glimpsed Valerie with her friends around school. At the park, spotting her wearing their school colors—a purple and gold beanie—he couldn't resist making a lasting impression.

As the photography group gathered around Valerie, who was busy adjusting the camera settings, Dev slyly crept up behind them and swiftly snatched Valerie's beanie from her head.

Startled, Valerie spun around and immediately broke away from her classmates, pursuing him into the playground. Meanwhile, her puzzled friends remained on the sidelines, watching the chase unfold.

Dev evaded Valerie's attempts to reclaim her beanie by twisting and turning around the playground sets and kicking up sand in every direction. Leading her to the open, grassy field, he dangled the beanie in front of her as she reached out, their laughter echoing in the air, captured for eternity by one of Valerie's classmates on their camera phone. On the second-to-last day of his freshman year, while flipping through his friend's yearbook as they cleared out their lockers, Dev stumbled upon their photo beneath a striking splash page titled "Lancer Moments." It revealed something hidden beneath their smiles, something more profound than shared laughter. When the winter formal finally arrived the following school year, Dev trusted his instincts and confidently asked Valerie to the dance during the middle of lunch. Valerie's enthusiastic "Yes!" began a relationship that bound them together through adolescent insecurities, desires, and the enchantment of first love.

Snapped back to reality by the torrential downpour, his cherished memories gave way to Veronica's relentless presence. Dev cleared his mind and adjusted his weight on the skateboard as the street curved before him like a slingshot. The rain intensified, descending with the force of blunt-tipped needles.

Dev's silhouette streaked past a closed elementary school. Its windows were shrouded in darkness, and the deserted playground served as a poignant reminder that the school would come alive in six hours with the hustle and bustle of students and teachers. He redirected his anxious thoughts of being exhausted in class and instead found himself admiring the towering golden arches of The Norwalk Square Tower. Its yellow arches, reminiscent of oil spurting from an oil well tower, captivated his attention. The building stood out as a city landmark, visible against any weather backdrop. From where Dev rode his skateboard, it rose above the rooftops like a sentinel, watching its residents and their doings.

Dev turned away just in time to discover a fully grown tree obstructing the middle of the road. He hit the brakes on his skateboard and hopped off. The fallen tree was wrapped in caution tape and surrounded by orange cones set up by public safety. Since the tree wasn't causing a traffic jam, chopping it into pieces would have to wait for a more favorable day.

Carefully, Dev passed the tree, observing its rigid roots that resembled otherworldly tentacles, covered in mud and grime, while raindrops fell within his field of vision. After passing it, he dashed to the middle of the road, eager to continue his journey. The streets were quiet and cold, with the chilly wind accompanying him throughout his long trek. On his left, the skateboard's wheels spun as he glided past another school. Dev marveled at how close he was to reaching her house. He only had a few more blocks to go. Adrenaline and confidence gave way to a sense of ease. Feeling relieved, Dev let out a long exhale.

The worn-out song he had contemplated changing lowered in volume as his back pocket vibrated. It was a text message. He debated whether to ignore it until he reached the entrance of the One Ways, where he could safely read the message. The irony of pondering safety while considering the dangerous One Ways wasn't lost on him. His pocket vibrated again. Valerie might have an urgent message for him.

Rolling into a different neighborhood, Dev reached for his back pocket and retrieved his phone. Adjusting his posture, he leaned over the screen. The raindrops made it challenging to read the glaring display, but he could make out the text message.

12:40 AM

VAL

I turned on the porch lite 4 - -

The skateboard wobbled uncontrollably beneath his feet. The rain damaged its wheel bearings. Dev was aware of the risks of skateboarding in such conditions, but he took the chance for her. Instinctively, he attempted to brake with his backfoot, but the slick pavement denied him a smooth stop. His backfoot twisted unnaturally to the side, accompanied by the unsettling sound of tendons popping.

"Ahhhh!!!" he cried out in pain.

The sudden jerk caused his phone to soar from his hand, yanking the earbuds out of his ears. He lunged forward, tumbling into the street, his poncho torn apart as it scraped against the rough asphalt. In mere moments, all his careful planning was undone. Dev came to a rolling halt near the rear wheel of a parked car. Gasping for breath, he lay motionless on the wet street as the rain poured on him.

~

A reading lamp clicked on beside a bedroom window, casting a gentle glow that illuminated the room, which was neither too bright nor too dim. Robert stepped away from his nightly routine, his gaze drawn to the drenched world outside the window, thinking of his brother. Dev had left an hour ago, leaving Robert restless and uneased; the cozy evening he had envisioned for himself had transformed into a night of regret. He should have stopped Dev. He should have made a deliberate, noisy disturbance to awaken their parents. But he didn't. He was a pushover, and he despised himself for it.

With a sigh, Robert turned away from the window and reached for his earbuds. He opened an app that led him to a saved radio station as he picked up his phone. Without the burden of morning responsibilities, he had become a nocturnal creature, relying on a radio show he had discovered on a late summer night to keep him company until sleep beckoned, usually just before dawn.

Robert settled back onto his bed, his head sinking into the plush pillow. Tonight, he needed to listen to "The Other Realm" more than ever. With his brother braving the elements, Robert couldn't find solace in slumber until Dev returned home. He glanced at his phone, hoping for a text message from his brother, but all he saw was the radio app playing on the screen. Disappointed, he placed the phone face down on the comforter.

"...calling from Norwalk, California. Welcome to the show. Do you have a name to share?" Johnny Decker's friendly voice inquired.

The caller immediately captured Robert's attention. Knowing that someone from his city was reaching out tonight made him feel less alone.

"No," the female caller responded, her voice trembling audibly. "I prefer to remain anonymous."

"Not a problem," Decker reassured her. "What would you like to ask Dolores Kingston?"

"Yes, Mrs. Kingston. I have a daughter, and I don't know what to do anymore. I'm at my wits' end."

"I'm sorry to hear that," Robert heard a soothing British voice reply to the distressed caller. "But I'm not sure how I can assist. I'm a demonologist."

"I know. You see, my daughter wakes up in the middle of the night screaming. She believes there's something in her closet. She says it wants to devour her. Her *night fits* are becoming...are becoming...I don't know what to do..."

Robert listened intently. The woman's words momentarily overshadowed his concerns about his brother's whereabouts.

~

Sprawled on the side of the street like a discarded ragdoll, Dev struggled to catch his breath while raindrops trickled down his scraped cheeks. The sound of rain enveloped him, and as he opened his eyes, he saw a glimpse of the swollen rain clouds unleashing their downpour upon him. Suddenly, a realization struck him.

"My phone!" he exclaimed, pushing himself up from the pavement with his arm. Bruised and battered, Dev winced as he rose to his feet. A sharp pain shot through his right ankle, causing him to let out a long gasp of air. The throbbing tendons created a kaleidoscope of flickering stars in his vision.

"Fuck..."

Bent over with his hands on his injured knee, Dev frantically searched for his phone, only to find his earbuds lying in the middle of the street. His skateboard, too, had rolled partially under a parked car from where he had fallen. His heart sank.

His phone glowed like a beacon beneath the water's surface in the flooded gutter, resembling an urban pond. Dev limped towards it, stopping at the edge of the gutter. Disheartened, he realized there was no straightforward way to retrieve his phone. With a grimace, he slowly inched his way towards it, his feet submerging into the icy water that seeped into his shoes and socks. Without wasting a moment, he rolled up his sleeve and swiftly retrieved his phone from the gutter. As he began to retreat, another jolt of pain surged through his sprained ankle. Dev fell backward onto the street but managed to hold his phone high above his face, preventing the screen from shattering against the pavement upon impact. It remained intact, but his phone was water-damaged, and his tailbone throbbed in discomfort.

Lying on the pavement with his feet near the gutter, Dev attempted to swipe his phone with a trembling finger. His desperate attempts proved futile as the device remained frozen. He could do nothing until the internal components dried out.

Feeling utterly unlucky, Dev gradually gathered his belongings. His skateboard, like his ankle, was in ruins. He ran his hand over the front wheels. They were loose in their tracks. Even if he hadn't injured himself, he couldn't ride it. He had no choice but to walk the rest of the way, a twenty-minute journey that seemed daunting with his hobbling injury. Another unknown fact nagged at him. How long would it take to walk back home with a sprained ankle? An eternity, he wagered. Hell, he might as well be dead before his parents could kill him first. Dev turned away from his skateboard and gazed at the wet road, contemplating the challenging journey ahead.

I've gone too far.

Not wanting to add unnecessary weight to the arduous remainder of his journey, Dev let go of his skateboard, letting it drop by his soaked shoes, and staggered forward, longing for Valerie's embrace. Despite the relentless showers, shifting winds, and the growing ache that forced Dev to pause multiple times during the trip, he persevered and hobbled to Cheshire Street's entrance. As he was about to venture into the heart of the beast, he glanced up and spotted a warning sign that read:

ONE WAY ONLY! DO NOT ENTER!

Dev turned away and hurriedly shuffled past the sign, letting out a sigh of relief. The rain had finally subsided to a drizzle, and Dev was immensely grateful for the respite.

Dev, desperate, repeated Valerie's address in his head.

661 ½...661 ½...661 ½.

He scanned both sides of the cramped, narrow street in his search for her house. Dev had never ventured into her neighborhood, aware of the inherent dangers of dating a Latina. Their relationship was taboo to many traditionalists who preferred to keep their cultures separate, and many lived in this neighborhood. Dev knew that one wrong step here could cost him his life. Standing in the middle of the one-way street, he felt exposed and uneasy, as if the tightly packed houses around him were scrutinizing his every move.

661 ½...661 ½.

He had found Valerie's third house before the street curved to the next block. The porch light was left on for him. Dev reached for his phone, attempting to unlock the screen, but it remained frozen. He approached the black gated fence with a limp and quickly opened it by turning the metal doorknob. Slowly stepping into the courtyard, Dev closed the gate behind him, savoring the scent of damp flowers that permeated the small space. He turned around and staggered to the porch, following the pathway adorned with vases filled with vibrant flowers.

Finally, Dev reached the foot of the door. Without a working phone, he was unsure whether to knock or enter. Hunching over and contemplating his next move, he realized he had no choice. He took a deep breath, closed his eyes, and knocked on the door. Dev waited for a moment but received no answer. His knock had been too brief and inconspicuous. She hadn't heard him. He knew he needed to be more assertive. Throwing his hoodie back, fabric, and plastic, he rapped on the door confidently.

Stepping back, he waited, and the seconds stretched before him, vast and silent, much like the emptiness and chill of the night. Once again, there was nothing but the sound of water dripping from the leaves of the plants behind him. He raised his hand, poised for another knock, but abruptly halted.

A hallway light flickered on, catching his attention through the living room window. Someone was awake, but was it Valerie? Lowering his arm, he heard approaching footsteps. His heart raced as he listened to the heavy locks being unlocked. When the door creaked open, he longed to be enveloped in Valerie's arms as he saw her curious brown eyes peering through the dimly lit foyer.

"Valerie..."

Realizing it was her boyfriend standing at her doorstep and not some crazed man roaming the wet streets, she opened the door for him.

"Dev!" She exclaimed, holding back her excitement and relief. Her expression changed as he hobbled his way inside. "Dev? Are you okay? What happened?"

"I sprained my ankle. I need to sit down."

"Babe," Valerie said, shutting the door. "You should have called your parents to pick you up."

"Even if I wanted to, I can't. My phone is busted." Dev glanced around the house, noticing photos of Valerie's family alongside portraits of Catholic saints adorning the living room. His attention returned to her as she took hold of his arm and wrapped it around her petite frame.

"Let's go to my room," she said, guiding him down a short hallway, one hop at a time. "Your hands are freezing," she commented as they reached her door. Leaning on Valerie for support, Dev entered her cozy and warm bedroom. She released her grip on him and went to close the door. Dev leaned against the sidewall, using it to maintain his balance.

"Sit on my bed," she suggested from behind him.

"But I'm wet," he protested.

"It's okay," she replied, gently closing the door.

It hurt to argue. Dev limped toward the bed, turned around, and collapsed onto the mattress.

"Shh, my grandma is sleeping."

"I thought you said you were alone."

"My grandma is always here," she stated matter-of-factly rather than with annoyance. "She won't bother us."

Dev instinctively shielded his eyes as she flicked on the lights, mimicking a vampire avoiding sunlight.

"How did you sprain it?" she asked, walking toward him.

"The rain messed up the bearings of my board. I wiped out. Bad." Now that his eyes had adjusted to the brightness, he could finally see her. She wore a long-sleeved pink pajama shirt with a chubby panda bear devouring a chocolate cupcake emblazoned on the front. The same panda adorned her leggings as well. Valerie looked cute in her outfit, causing Dev to blush.

"Take them off," she said casually.

"What?" Dev replied awkwardly.

"Take off your shoes," Valerie clarified, giving him a warm smile. She understood how her words might have sounded to him. "Let's see how bad it is," she said.

Dev composed himself and wiped the beads of water off his face. He effortlessly grabbed his uninjured foot, removed his shoe, and soaked his sock, dropping them to the floor. They both observed that his foot was damp and wrinkled but otherwise unharmed. His sprained foot, however, had him gritting his teeth as he attempted to remove his other shoe. Helplessly, Dev shook his head and said, "I can't." Sniffling and shivering, he gently lowered his sprained foot back down.

Valerie got down on one knee and placed her hands on his soaked shoe without asking.

"Ready?" she asked, looking up at him from below.

Dev took a deep breath, nervously nodding.

Valerie carefully removed his tightly laced shoe from his swollen ankle as if his foot had transformed into a delicate eggshell. Trembling, he clutched her bed's comforter, leaning back. Dev closed his eyes and tilted his head back in anticipation. A sigh of relief escaped his lips as he finally felt the shoe slide off. Loosening his grip on the comforter, which was nothing more than a blanket draped over the mattress, he said with a sweaty brow, "I think I can--"

Valerie peeled back his sock, and once again, he clutched the blanket, bracing himself for the excruciating pain. However, it didn't come. His girl possessed the touch of an angel. She uncovered his foot with gentle ease. He felt nothing but the cool air caressing his exposed, stiff toes. The tension in his shoulders eased until...

"Oh, babe." Valerie recoiled from what she saw.

Furrowing his brow, Dev examined his ankle. It was a swollen, purple mass that needed immediate medical attention. He had taken spills and wipeouts on his skateboard before but had never injured himself to this degree, which troubled him.

"You need to go to the emergency room," he heard her say.

"I'll be alright," Dev replied, more to convince himself than her. He gingerly rotated his stiff ankle and winced from the strain. Valerie was right. He needed to see a doctor. But at that moment, all he wanted was to stay with her.

"Dev..."

"I don't want to get you in trouble," he explained, studying her eyes. "And I don't want to go."

A heavy silence settled between them, broken only by the howling wind rattling the bedroom window. Valerie turned away from his gaze and finally noticed that he was completely drenched from head to toe. During the hectic commotion of getting Dev safe inside her room, she hadn't realized how thoroughly soaked his pants and sleeves had become in the rain. She knew what she had to do.

Valerie rose from the bed and said, "Your foot needs to be wrapped up. My grandma..." Valerie smiled, recognizing that a demonstration would be more effective. "It'll only take a second, okay?"

Dev asked as she headed for the door, "Can I borrow your phone?"

She turned to him, listening intently.

"I need to text my brother. He needs to know I made it here, okay." Dev cracked a nervous smirk. "Well, sort of okay."

Valerie reached into her pajama pocket and retrieved her phone. She tossed it to Dev, who caught it with one hand. "The Password is 7799," she informed him before leaving the room.

Feverishly typing the password, he swiftly accessed Valerie's text messaging app. Dev then entered his brother's number, which he knew by heart because Robert's phone number ended with a digit one higher than his own. He proceeded to type in the message field:

1:30 AM

Hey, man. It's me. I made it. I busted my phone. I'm OK.

Dev sent his message without giving it a second glance. Gripping the phone tightly, he placed it face down on the blanket and shifted his attention to his baseball-sized ankle. It felt rigid and warm. How the hell was he going to make it back home? The thought of it made his stomach turn. Suddenly, he felt the phone vibrate in his hand. He swiftly brought it up and eagerly read:

1:31 AM

UNKNOWN NUMBER

Bummer. Text me when you leave.

1:32 AM

KK

Shivering, Dev quickly locked Valerie's phone just as she entered the room. In her hands, he noticed something folded beneath a roll of bandages and a small bottle of cream, but he couldn't quite make out what it was.

"Before I wrap your foot, I need you to change out of your wet clothes. I brought my dad's sweats for you to wear," Valerie said, placing the items on a cramped desk next to an old, hand-me-down bookshelf.

"Won't he notice them missing?" Dev questioned, his plastic poncho rustling as he moved. Valerie turned her head to see what he was doing and observed him struggling to reach his feet. Concerned, she approached him and extended her arm for support. Dev reached for it but missed, falling back onto the mattress.

"Be careful," Valerie cautioned.

Leveraging her weight with the heels of her feet, Valerie pulled him off the bed. Dev stood before her, a bit exasperated, resembling a flamingo with his injured foot dangling slightly off the ground. At that moment, they gazed into each other's eyes, lost in their connection. Valerie stood on her tiptoes, closed her eyes, and planted a long kiss on his lips, washing away the hardships of his night into the flooded gutters.

They broke away from their kiss and opened their eyes together.

Dev softly spoke, "Do you want to leave the room while I change?"

"What if you need my help?" Valerie replied, the truth of her desire evident in her eyes. The last thing she wanted was to leave his side.

Understanding her unspoken wish, Dev nodded. He noticed her blush, but she didn't turn away from him.

While Dev peeled off the tattered plastic poncho that had kept his upper body somewhat dry, Valerie grabbed her father's gray thermal from the desk. Dev took off his sweatshirt as she turned around to hand him the oversized thermal. She had only seen him in a tank top a few times during the summer, and now, with his slender stomach exposed in her room as he stretched his arms upward, revealing his bony ribcage and outie bellybutton, Valerie couldn't help but blush once more.

Unaware of his girl's admiration for his body, Dev casually dropped his sweatshirt on top of his brother's makeshift poncho. Shirtless, he placed on the thermal she handed him.

"Jesus, it's like I lost a million pounds," he joked, playfully extending his arms to showcase the oversized thermal. They shared a laugh, the first of the night.

"My dad's a big guy," Valerie commented.

"I can see that," Dev replied with a smile.

Valerie picked up her father's sweatpants and said, "These are from when my dad was a bit thinner. If you tie the string several times, they should be tight enough for you to wear."

Dev released the notch on his belt and shifted his hips from side to side. His waterlogged jeans immediately loosened, sagged, and dropped to his feet. The weight of the bulky pants landed on his sprained ankle, causing him to flinch. Valerie moved to catch him without hesitation as he fell back onto the mattress. Suppressing his cries with closed eyes, Dev heard her concerned voice ask, "Are you okay?"

"I need your help," Dev admitted, breaking into sweat-induced pain. "I'm sorry, babe."

Valerie approached him and paused by his feet, where his pants had fallen. She threw her father's sweatpants over her shoulder and knelt beside him, gently shimmying off Dev's wet jeans. Fearful that Valerie might accidentally move his sprained foot in the wrong direction, Dev disregarded that he was now in his boxer shorts in front of her. What could have been an awkward moment turned into relief as she skillfully removed his jeans without causing him any pain. Leaning back against the bed with his elbows supporting his weight, he watched as she carefully placed her father's baggy sweatpants on him.

Once done, Valerie stood up and asked, "Can you pull them up?"

Dev nodded, grateful for her help, and proceeded to pull up the sweatpants, adjusting them as best he could.

While Dev settled onto the mattress again, Valerie brought over the last remaining items from the desk—a roll of bandages and a jar of ointment labeled in Spanish.

"I need you to lay on my pillow," she instructed, switching on the reading lamp on the nearby nightstand.

Dev followed her directions, feeling a chill run down his neck as his head touched the pillow. He watched Valerie make her way to the shut door, turning off the lights and enveloping them in near darkness. Carefully, she walked back to the bed and climbed onto the far end of the mattress using her knees. Their faces were both halfway covered in shadows, creating an intimate mood.

"Can you give me my kitty pillow right by you?" she asked.

Dev turned to his side and spotted the pink cartoon kitty pillow conveniently placed near his head. He grabbed it by its rabbit-sized ears protruding from its round pillowcase and handed it to her.

With his curiosity piqued, Dev asked, "What are you doing?"

Cautiously, Valerie lifted his swollen ankle and positioned his foot underneath her kitty pillow. As she did so, Dev felt his throbbing foot begin to stiffen.

"I'm going to make you feel better," she replied gently.

Valerie scooped up a handful of green ointment. Its pungent smell immediately reached Dev's nostrils.

"That stuff stinks," Dev remarked with a childish frown.

"It's supposedly made from snakes," she said, applying the ointment to her palms before gently massaging his sprained ankle with strength and care.

Anxious, Dev gripped the blanket tightly as Valerie's hands found his injured foot's twisted knots and swollen tendons. But soon, he discovered the soothing sensation of both the cooling and warming ointment, causing him to relax his grip and inquire, "Have you done this before?"

Valerie smiled and confessed that she had only done it a few times. Her abuelita, her grandmother, was known as a holistic healer in the family. She had recently started sharing their family's trade secrets with Valerie as she came of age. One of the first lessons her abuelita taught her was to divert the patient's attention from their pain, which she did by telling Dev a story about a clumsy cousin who frequently sprained his ankle and sought their grandmother's help for relief. While Valerie shared her experiences helping her grandmother, her sturdy and lubricated fingers continued their gentle massages on his torn tendon. The pressure she applied kept his gasps to a minimum. As she deftly maintained the conversation, she pulled out a red bandana from her pajama pants pocket and started cracking each of his toes, starting with the pinky toe. She wiped her hands clean with the rag, then wrapped his ankle tightly with the bandana. Pausing her story about her cousin, she finished his treatment by carefully elevating his bandaged foot onto her kitty pillow.

Dev was astonished by Valerie's quick and attentive care. He watched with heavy, tired eyes as she approached him, resting her head on an empty pillow beside him. They moved in for a kiss. Their wet lips moved in sync as the gentle rain outside created a soft melody.

Suddenly, Dev winced, breaking their passionate kiss. The ointment on his ankle had triggered a chemical reaction, making his foot feel warm. He pulled away from Valerie's lips and confessed, "My foot is burning."

Valerie shifted her body into a fetal position and faced him. "Yeah, that's normal. It would help if you stayed off your feet for a few days," she said. With her elbow propped on the mattress and palm cradling her cheek, she added, "Dev, how the hell are you going to make it home?"

Dev pondered momentarily and replied, "There are worse things that could have happened to me tonight. A sprained ankle is the least of my worries." He tried to shift into the same fetal position as Valerie, but she firmly held him down with her free hand.

"Don't move," she said. "You have to keep your foot elevated."

Settling back on the bed, Dev wrapped his arm around her shoulders as she nestled her head on his arm. He could hear her breathing, and she could hear his heartbeat. They let the stillness hang between them, but not for too long.

"I'm glad you made it," she said softly.

"Me too."

As Valerie leaned closer, Dev closed his eyes and pulled her in for the kisses he had been yearning for all night. Their passionate kisses soothed his chapped, cracked lips. Swept up in the heat of the moment yet mindful of his elevated foot, Valerie slowly positioned herself on top of him. Even with her gentle touch, she inadvertently jostled the mattress. Suppressing his pain, he pulled away. Wincing, she touched his chest and said, "I'm sorry."

Biting his lip, Dev replied, "It's all right."

Dev gradually felt his muscles relax as he settled back into bed. Gently, he cradled her face in his hands, and Valerie leaned in for another series of gentle kisses. His thumb grazed her lips as he breathed in her sweet scent, drowning his lungs with its fragrance. He pecked her lips once, then, with his face pressed close to hers, he kissed his way along the curve of her smooth, naked neck. He nibbled on her skin. For the first time in their relationship, beneath her trembling breath, he heard her moan. Fueled by her whimpers, Dev wrapped a strong arm around Valerie's waist, moving his hips in perfect harmony with hers.

As a new wave of rain showers fell outside, Valerie, flustered, pushed herself away from him. Sweating and arching her back, she reached for his manhood, which was covered by her father's sweatpants. In the throes of anticipation for what lay ahead, Dev reclined on the pillow and watched her as she pleasured him. Their intense gazes never wavered from one another. With each stroke she made, he felt himself getting closer to--

"Take them off," she whispered.

Dev gulped hard and wiggled the sweatpants down to his knees as Valerie leaned forward, allowing him to slip them off. Once he was done, she sat back on top of him and reached behind to touch his naked arousal. It was a sensation he had never experienced before, and her touch felt unfamiliar and incredibly pleasurable. Biting his lower lip, this time from pleasure, Dev's mind raced with the decision of how to proceed with their lovemaking. Hormones coursed through his veins, fueled by his attraction to her and their shared desires. He brought his hands to the waistline of her pajama pants and pulled them down to her knees, with Valerie assisting in the process. His hand then caressed her thigh, and as he did so, his gaze lingered on her while his fingers inched closer to her wet entrance, which he felt exposed against his flat belly. Dev watched her shudder as his fingers explored her most intimate place, and her moans blended with the sound of raindrops falling outside the window.

Drawing back his hand, Dev continued to stroke her bare thighs gently. "We don't have to if you don't want to. I'm perfectly fine with us just doing this."

Valerie's eyes shifted to the window, and there was a brief pause before she returned her gaze to Dev. "I'm a little scared. I've heard it hurts."

"I've heard the same thing," Dev admitted. "If it hurts too much, we can stop."

Valerie nodded, awkwardly guiding him into the most intimate space. Dev could only feel himself prodding around, not experiencing much sensation. Contrary to all the locker room conversations he had heard, the anticipation of his first time was losing its mystique.

Is this how it's supposed to feel?

His uncertainty disappeared as he penetrated her, causing Valerie to shut her eyes with a pained wince on her face. She tilted her head slightly to the side, resting her hand on his chest. As she opened her eyes, she looked down at Dev, observing his considerate and cautious movements as he pleasured her, ensuring her comfort throughout.

Her moans grew more exotic and intense, filled with heated passion. Dev placed his hands on her hips, swaying their hips in harmony like an anchored boat. As he reached up beneath her thin pajama shirt, he grabbed a handful of her firm and tight breasts. Sensing her hardened nipples, he gently played with them.

In an instant, just as Valerie was about to take off her shirt, a pickup truck pulled into the gated fence. Its bright headlights pierced through the drawn curtains, casting contrasting light and shadows across their startled bodies.

"Shit! It's my dad!" Valerie said in a panic.

"What?!" Dev slipped out from inside her as she quickly moved away. He pulled up her father's sweatpants and tied the string into a knot with one fluid motion. "I thought he was supposed to be at work?" Dev replied, using his elbows to push himself off the bed.

Meanwhile, Valerie got off the bed, holding her pants. She turned to him and said with disappointment, "The rain."

Dev hated that she was right. The rain had caused him many problems on his way to Valerie's place. The downpour had turned gutters into ponds, and debris from Veronica's wrath was scattered everywhere, making the streets treacherous. He imagined the freeways were now vast lagoons, making it impossible for anyone to drive through.

"Damn," Dev muttered under his breath. Carefully lifting his sprained ankle off the kitty pillow, he lumbered off the bed, feeling every movement in his tender tendons. As the bulky metal pickup truck door creaked open, Valerie placed her arm around Dev's waist while the fence was pushed open at the far end of its track.

"Should I hide in the closet?" Dev asked, his voice trembling with panic.

"There's no room," Valerie replied. Desperately, she scanned her room for a hiding place for Dev. Her eyes landed on the small gap underneath the bedframe.

"Under the bed?" She asked him.

"If it keeps your dad from killing me."

Valerie painstakingly guided him under the bed. She stood back, watching him wiggle into the dark space beneath the bed frame.

Sliding his wet clothes with him, she apologetically said, "I'm so sorry."

"It's okay," Dev reassured her, "You didn't know."

Under the dusty corner of the bed, Dev reached his hand out for her. She held it tightly, their fingers interlocking. He squeezed her hand gently, silently reassuring her that everything would be all right. The pickup truck echoed ominously in the driveway as it entered. "We'll be okay, Val." Dev then whispered what he truly believed, "I love you."

~

The rain finally let up at twenty minutes past three, but the winds continued to howl fiercely across the city. Bundled up in his gray hoodie, Dev limped along a dimly lit sidewalk on a main street. Despite his attempts to stay warm, he shivered uncontrollably, tucking his hands under his armpits. After they heard her dad snoring in his bedroom, it had been thirty minutes since he left Valerie's place. The biting wind reminded him of the reality of his journey back home. His skateboard was gone, his foot throbbed in pain, and worst of all, he had four and a half miles to cover before reaching the safety and warmth of his room. The trek to Longworth Avenue seemed impossible in the dead of night.

Valerie had begged him to stay the night with her, but he knew the consequences if they were caught. Despite his better judgment, he assured her that he would be fine. It wouldn't be easy, but he would manage. Before limping away, he instructed her to text his brother that he was on his way home. Now, hobbling along Pioneer Boulevard, he wished there was another option.Dev shrugged his shoulders and looked ahead. He spotted the glowing golden arches rising above the city's town center tower. It was just a few blocks away, but he was already exhausted. His sprained ankle felt stiff, and he could only hobble forward using his heel, covering just a few feet at a time. He hadn't even gone a mile, and blisters were already forming on his feet.

Suddenly, a vehicle sped up behind him, its sirens emitting a brief, sharp sound. Dev quickly stopped as the black and white car pulled beside him in the oncoming lane. The officer inside the vehicle directed a blinding spotlight at Dev from his window. Instinctively, Dev raised his hand to shield his eyes from the harsh glare.

"Let me see your face," the officer commanded while simultaneously reporting the stop to dispatch through his mobile radio intercom.

"What?" Dev replied, squinting against the blinding light that obscured the officer's features. At that moment, the officer appeared more like a shadowy silhouette than a distinct figure.

"You heard what I said," the officer repeated. "Do it."

Dev pulled back his hoodie, trembling as he turned to face the officer.

The officer scanned him up and down and asked, "Were you discharged from College State Hospital?"

Confused, Dev responded, "What's that?"

"Displaced?"

"I don't know what that means."

"Where are you from, kid?"

"I live on Longworth Avenue. I... I was visiting my girl-friend."

"Girlfriend?" the officer asked.

"Could you give me a ride home? I sprained my ankle on my way to her place. My skateboard is busted."

"I'm not a taxi, kid."

"I know, but..." The muffled voice from dispatch inter-rupted Dev's words.

"What's your name, kid?" the officer finally asked.

"Devell Lewis," Dev answered, his breath forming a frosty cloud in the cold air. "But everyone calls me Dev."

Once again, the officer remained silent. The dispatch's voice crackled over the radio, urging the officer to respond.

Dev heard a click as the officer answered the call. "Nothing. Continuing patrol. Over."

Watching the black and white cruiser speed away, Dev was surprised when it abruptly made a sharp U-turn and headed back toward him. The officer rolled down the automatic window, revealing his face to a dazed and bewildered Dev.

"Get in the back," the officer commanded, his face still hidden in the shadows.

Dev didn't question the officer's orders and went to the back passenger door reserved for troublemakers.

"Longworth?" the officer asked.

"Yeah. Turn around and keep--"

"I know where that is."

With a swift U-turn, the cruiser sped up the street. Its flashing red and blue lights served as a warning as the officer bypassed the empty intersection. The rest of the drive to Dev's home remained uninterrupted by dispatch.

Ignoring Dev's request to be dropped off at the street corner, the sheriff dropped him right in front of his house. The cruiser remained parked until Dev had safely entered his home.

Later in the morning, as his parents' alarm clock filled their bedroom, he found himself nestled in his warm bed. Having changed into clean pajamas, he wrapped himself in a thick, cozy blanket while propping up his sprained ankle on a pillow.

As he lay there, he replayed the night's events, contemplating their significance for him and Valerie. Did Valerie's father intentionally remain silent as Dev hobbled away? Had her father scolded her after he had left? Even though their intimate moment had been short, were they still considered virgins? And what would he tell his parents when they returned from work and discovered he hadn't gone to school due to a sprained ankle from his late-night escapade? As dawn broke and Dev drifted off, he realized he had no answers. Yet, one thing remained true: his profound love for Valerie.

The memory of Valerie and their unforgettable stormy night with Veronica would endure, a beacon of light amongst life's most uncertain storms.

Dustin Howard

ustin Howard brooded over his rum and coke as an arctic blue stage light illuminated the machine shop that was transformed into Santa's Village. From his vantage point, he observed his former colleagues, whom he considered a bunch of imbeciles, clumsily dancing to the tunes of a cover band audacious enough to butcher the classic rock songs he cherished. It was a painful sight to see.

Dustin, a magnet for conflict and despised by many of his peers, downed his drink with the same vigor he had displayed while consuming the five previous alcoholic beverages. The band, aptly named "Teenage Waste Band," managed to inject some life back into the party around nine o'clock, but even that couldn't lift Dustin's spirit. In a single gulp, he drowned his frustration.

Secretly, and certainly not something he would ever admit, Dustin couldn't deny the undeniable talent of the lead guitarist. The brat—dressed in a slim blue velvet suit and a thin black tie—was not only flawlessly playing the chords on his glossy red electric guitar but also infusing the vocals with a spirited passion that reminded Dustin of his youth. Back in the day, before he became a grizzled old man and burdened with the care of his mentally challenged nephew, he and his '79 Datsun ruled the night as rebellious masters of the streets.

Ironically, the song the snowflake band chose to perform seemed tailor-made to mock his current situation—an unapologetic middle finger aimed squarely at him. They were rocking out to "*The Breakup Song.*"

Feeling the liquor slide down his throat, leaving behind a faint taste of flat soda on his tongue, Dustin shrugged.

What does that fucking brat know about the words he's singing?

Pushing his glasses to his forehead, Dustin continued scrutinizing the extravagant waste of money. It was the company's annual Christmas party, coincidentally the final one to be held at the shop before Caltrans demolished its dilapidated walls. Edward Shultz, the machine shop owner's son, spared no expense on an "end of the year" extravaganza for his dedicated employees, knowing his father's shop was coming to its end.

The petting zone outside the parking lot captivated the children, which would soon make way for a new on-ramp to the I-5 freeway in the coming years. Inside the shop, the adults reveled in the highly anticipated barbecue catering that had sparked excitement among the machinists all week leading up to the festivities. And, naturally, there was an open bar to quench the thirst of the enthusiastic drinkers.

Behind the fireplace countertop, the bartender dressed as one of Santa's elves served various beers, wines, and spirits. One might assume that all these festivities would have lifted Dustin's sour mood, but instead, they only amplified his Scrooge-like and downcast demeanor.

What a waste of money.

The fake snow machine kicked in, transforming the lively scene into a magical winter wonderland.

Yeah, let the snowflakes rain on the snowflakes.

Dustin turned around to face the elf bartender, who was conveniently within arm's reach. Placing his clear plastic cup on the countertop, he looked up at the bartender through his crooked glasses and shouted, "Make it louder than them!"

The elf bartender, well acquainted with Dustin's preferences because he never strayed far from his side, immediately made his rum and coke. As he waited, Dustin fidgeted in his worn brown leather jacket, causing tiny fragments of material to chip off and drift to the ground. Years ago, during a lunch break, as Dustin stood up from the table, his jacket left a trail of dust behind him. It caught the attention of the young machinists who sat nearby. One of the wisecracking men quickly added, "That foo' is dusty, dawg! Dusty Dustin!" The lunch room erupted with laughter. Since that moment, any newcomers entering the shop, whom Dustin held in low regard and had a long list of derogatory names for, only knew him as "Dusty."

The bartender placed his drink on the countertop. He took the drink and savored it. The beverage sang with the spirit of Friday night madness—the kind that fueled weekend warriors like Dustin Howard, whose thirst was never quenched.

Ready to embark on his usual path of self-destructive mischief, Dustin left the oblivious elf without uttering a word of gratitude. His legs, numbed by alcohol, carried him across the concrete dance floor toward the corner of the building for the final time. Through the artificial snow that drifted on him, he caught sight of the lone piece of equipment purposely left behind—the essence of his livelihood, *his* numerical control machine.

The clunky NC Machine, a relic from an era when all things electrical were encased in cast iron, emerged from the shadows, shrouding Dustin from the bustling party. The instant he approached it, the scent of oil and freshly shaved metal engulfed the air. It was a familiar smell that Dustin loved. Despite the shop's lack of machinery, his workstation retained the essence of forty years of repetitive steel casting labor. Gone were the days when he could seek solace behind his workstation, the one place where people would leave him alone. Despite being sixty-five years old, Dustin relished the comfort of solitude.

With the machine shop relocating, Eddie finally found a reason to push Dustin into early retirement. When Dustin received the news that he wouldn't be joining them in the new year, his fury went beyond mere anger—he was practically foaming at the mouth in disbelief and betrayal. Even the generous pension fund couldn't soothe the feeling of being stabbed in the back by the son of the man who had hired him all those years ago.

Placing his drink on the flat surface of a circular steel bed, Dustin's thoughts turned to the past. "I wish you were still around, Walt," he muttered silently. As the cover band's rendition of *"The Breakup Song"* ended, the oblivious partygoers clapped like trained seals.

Standing in the darkness, hunched over the antiquated machine that would soon end up in the junkyard come Monday morning, Dustin relived the night he first met Walter Shultz.

~

It was 1977, Memorial Day weekend in Norwalk. Dustin and his younger sister Lucy, accompanied by her pocket protector-wearing accountant boyfriend, decided to venture into a bar infamous for its rowdy patrons—Bobo's. With a neon sign by the roadside depicting a grinning, stout clown donning a bowler cap and an oversized white polka-dotted red bowtie, it came as no surprise Bobo's attracted booze hounds seeking juiced-up mayhem in its wooden-furnished tavern.

Dustin fondly recalled that night, which comprised three of his most cherished elements: rock' n' roll, easy women, and cheap drinks.

However, Dustin's luck with the ladies took a nosedive after an awkward game of pool, which ended with him losing twenty bucks and any chance of scoring with one of the dirty blondes he had been eyeing since he entered the bar. The strawberry farmer, or the Mexican day laborer, effortlessly out-played him like the three other poor saps who believed they could outsmart the guy who resembled Ricky Ricardo but played pool like Eddie Felson.

"God damn it!" Dustin shouted in frustration, throwing the cue onto the green cloth as the eight-ball sunk into the left corner pocket. He then pulled a twenty-dollar bill from his pants pocket, slamming it onto a nearby table before storming away.

"Good game, muchacho!" shouted the Ricky Ricardo look-alike, followed by laughter from the girls watching the game.

Dustin overheard Lucy's turd of a boyfriend, Richard, and asked, "Mind if I give it a go?"

Feeling emasculated and parched, Dustin slumped onto a recently vacated barstool. He pushed his glasses up and sig-naled the bartender for a drink, but those sons of bitches—both of 'em—were too busy attending to other customers to notice Dustin.

"When you get their attention, I'll buy you your drink," a husky voice spoke beside him.

Suspicious that a stranger, let alone another man, would offer to buy him a drink, Dustin turned his head to face the source of the voice. He scrutinized the man from his bulging belly to his green eyes, set within a moon pie face adorned with craters and dents. Sporting a navy-colored blazer and a blue button-up shirt, the man appeared to be a traveling salesman who had enjoyed a prosperous week and was now looking to spend his earnings.

"Keep your money. I have my own," Dustin replied irritably.

"I ain't coming on to you, son. I saw your game. Losing twenty bucks is tough. Let this round be on me."

Dustin hesitated, still not fully convinced of the stranger's generosity.

Sensing this, the pudgy man said, "Well, how about you get the next round?"

Dustin cracked a grin. "Then, I'll take a Budweiser."

The stranger in the navy blazer quickly brought his fingers to his lips and let out an ear-piercing whistle. It caught the bartender's attention, along with almost every drunk fool in the bar.

"A Whiskey on the rocks and a Budweiser, my good sir!" he shouted.

The bartender nodded.

With their orders in progress, the stranger extended his hefty hand and said, "Walter Schultz."

Shaking Walter's hand, which had a firm and tight grip, Dustin responded,

"Dustin Howard."

"Dustin, I see you're a man with a temper just as strong as your thirst for a drink," Walter remarked.

"What the hell is that supposed to mean?"

As the bartender placed their drinks in front of them, they both held them, waiting for the right moment to raise a toast. However, Dustin's blunt question hung in the air, creating an awkward moment.

"It means you've got to relax, son. So, what if you lost that game to that spic? In the grand scheme of things, you are the one who is winning. The world outside this bar, with all its opportunities, belongs to us. It always has and it always will."

"Amen, brother," Dustin sincerely said. He clinked his mug against Walter's whiskey glass, and they both took a drink.

"What's your line of business?" Walter set his glass down and pulled out a pack of Embassy cigarettes from his blazer's breast pocket.

"I work at a fat rendering plant in Vernon. It sucks," Dustin replied.

"Where do you see yourself in five years?" Walter lit his cigarette with a match, filling the air with the scent of sulfur. He offered one to Dustin, but Dustin declined.

"I want to make more money. I don't care how I do it, but it needs to happen in less than five years."

Walter took a drag of his cigarette, blowing out the smoke before asking, "Why? Do you have a family to support?"

Dustin scoffed and replied, "Once a man has a wife and some brats, he's never free. I like my freedom. And my money."

Dustin drank his drink, and Walter smiled.

"I like your bluntness, Dustin. I love it. As a married man with some brats of my own, I can relate to what you just said. But that doesn't stop me from having a good time. It's like what I told Sally, 'If you have a problem with it, you know where to find the door'."

"Did she give you any lip?" Dustin asked and then drank some more.

"Only where it counts," Walter replied, nudging him with a wink. The humor nearly caused Dustin to spit out his beer in laughter.

Walter's crude remarks earned Dustin's friendship. Sitting up straight, he wiped his mouth with the back of his hand and laughed. The ice had finally been broken between them.

"And what do you do for a living?" Dustin sincerely asked. After all, Walter was his new friend.

"I run a machine shop on Firestone Boulevard, near the 5 freeway."

When Walter introduced himself to Dustin, the last name struck a chord, but it didn't register until now. He snapped his fingers and exclaimed, "Shultz Machine Shop!"

Walter nodded, acknowledging Dustin's recognition, and tipped his glass in approval.

"Oh, man. I used to date a girl in Buena Park. I saw your company's sign every time I drove to her apartment. It always caught my eye because it's just a piece of scrap metal with the shop's name on it."

"Well, in the years to come, that's going to change. You see, my old man passed away recently, leaving me his shop and some of his debt, which wasn't much. I'm looking to fill a few positions because we're going to have a lot of work in the upcoming weeks. Are you interested?"

"Hell yeah!"

"Are you trainable?"

"I would say so."

"Can you come in on Tuesday morning, say eight o'clock, and fill out an application?"

"Absolutely!" Dustin was elated.

A night meant to be about getting wasted, he had unexpectedly landed a new job. He didn't know what he would be doing, but anything would be better than scrubbing blood and shit off the concrete floors. Screw that rendering plant. As for not showing up to work on that Tuesday or the following days, that was Dustin's way of sending a passive-aggressive message to the National Fat Renders of America that he was done. In the two weeks it took National to cut him his last paycheck—a whopping sixty dollars for forty-five hours of back-breaking, putrid work—Dustin had learned and retained the skills necessary to operate the newly acquired, albeit overly outdated now, NC machine.

Of course, there were some early mishaps.

About two months into his new job as a machinist, when Dustin felt confident enough to operate the numerical machine on his own, a batch of "simple t-hinges"—two barrels full—turned out to be inaccurate. The shop's foreman, Tim Tumbler, discovered the manufacturing flaw. Armed with his trusty caliper, silver on the level with red tips on its black clamps, Tim spot-checked the quality of Dustin's work and was aggravated to find that the t-hinges were flawed.

Having been out of high school for a few years without any college experience, Dustin's math skills, particularly in algebra, were a bit rusty. He understood the formulas and knew how to input the programs on punch cards to make the numerical machine produce the required workload for the day. However, if his equations were slightly off—which happened in that muggy July—it significantly affected how the steel material was cut and how long it took him to manually rewrite the code.

Despite Dustin's errors, of which there were a handful, Walter never lost his temper. He knew that Dustin's mistakes only made him stronger as a machinist, and his intuition proved correct. Dustin's slip-ups gradually became an anomaly and were no longer a significant issue. Even showing up to work hungover didn't affect Dustin's job performance. Well, except for him being a bit temperamental the next day, which became part of his personality as the decades went by. Despite a heavy night of drinking, Dustin would still arrive on time and perform his tasks flawlessly, and his skills didn't go unnoticed.

Under Walter's guidance, Dustin's wages increased each year, and during this period, lasting until the mid-80s, a series of self-indulgent splurges began. The first of these splurges was a brown leather jacket that could have been plucked straight out of the 1950s.

Driving up Firestone Boulevard in his hand-me-down Dodge Wagon, Dustin would often pass a row of retail stores on his way to work. Among them, one shop caught his eye. Behind its display window stood a mannequin wearing a slick, tough jacket that seemed to radiate under the morning sunlight. Every day, he imagined himself in that jacket. Certainly, it would attract the ladies' attention at the bars.

In February of '79, on a Friday, a week after Dustin received a fifty-cent pay raise, he made his fantasy a reality. He walked into the clothing shop, *Stylin' 4 Now,* and was greeted by a brunette girl with thunderous thighs named Jackie. He told her what he wanted and requested a medium size. Jackie informed him that the only medium they had left was on the display model, to which he had no objections.

In front of a dresser mirror near the fitting room, Jackie placed the Fonzie-esque jacket on Dustin. Seeing it on himself brought a delighted smile that veered into a sly grin. He admired the knit waistband and cuffs that brought out a nostalgic vibe, a time he wished he had experienced. However, what sealed the deal wasn't just his fondness for the '50s. It was the hunger in Jackie's eyes. The jacket was already doing its job of attracting the ladies, and after a brief exchange that didn't involve a commission-driven sale, she led him to her manager's office.With the price tag still attached to the sleeve, Dustin wore the $70 leather imitation jacket as he railed Jackie on a cluttered desk covered in yellow carbon copy invoices. For ten minutes, his hands rested on her thunderous thighs. Soon, her squeals were drowned out by the roaring sound of an inline-six engine and the opening guitar sequence of Blue Öyster Cult's rock classic, "Burnin' for You." From the jacket, a new memory was paved.

Freshly threaded tires of a newly polished gray 280ZX Datsun tore through a dark, narrow canyon road, illuminated only by the bug-eyed projector-like headlights. Music blared from the four-speaker radio system inside the cabin as the wind tangled Dustin's hair in knots and wild swirls. The orange glow of the dashboard lights shone upon him as he pushed his glasses up and shifted into third gear, paying no mind to anyone or anything.

Dustin's 1979 Datsun, his metallic steed, arrived sooner than his next annual raise. Sure, his "leather" jacket fed his inflated ego, but if he wanted to earn the respect of the boys—which he did—he needed a bitchin' ride.

The 280ZX was that bitchin' ride.

After scouring the dealerships of Cerritos Auto Square, a bustling hub devoted to new and used cars of all makes and models, Dustin stumbled upon the wax-polished beauty just as he was about to throw in the towel. She wasn't tucked away in a flashy showroom or placed on the curbside like a common sight. No, she held her ground amid the second row, sur-rounded by a procession of stationary Nissan models. As the autumn sunset painted the sky with streaks of red and purple, extending across the layered clouds on the horizon, Dustin couldn't help but envision how she would look tearing through the night roads. Picturing it sent shivers down his arms, causing goosebumps to sprout.

He desired her, and after a test drive that felt more like a formality than anything else, she became his, leaving his dull station wagon behind as a partial down payment.

With a determined destination in mind, Dustin's 280ZX burst out of the dealership like a beast awakening from a long, undisturbed slumber. With this purpose finally realized, its engine roared triumphantly as it sped underneath the freeway underpass.

Dustin had a two-day grace period with her. He could return her if she didn't meet his expectations, with a full refund and no questions asked. Not being a patient man, he didn't intend to waste two days figuring out if he wanted to keep the damn thing for the next sixty months. No way. He needed to take her where he knew all the young enthusiasts took their hot rides to race for glorious, competitive pride.

Turnbull Canyon Road.

From Whittier to Hacienda Heights, Turnbull Canyon Road connected both neighboring cities via a narrow, two-way, four-mile loop road. Scenic by day but treacherous by night, the canyon's curved hillsides and jagged boulders made even experienced drivers anxious due to its lack of roadside assistance. Few dared to approach due to the potential danger of crashing through the wooden barriers separating the cliff from the road, alongside rumors of potential satanic rituals in its hidden hillsides. However, none of these fears intimidated Dustin as much as the fear of being labeled a coward did.

Dustin was an intermediate racer who had always wanted to tackle the canyon road alone. Since Dustin and his high school buddy Jake first discovered the steep highway in Jake's night-black '69 GTO, their Friday nights had been about cruising.

For them, it often meant venturing onto the secluded back roads of Turnbull Canyon Road to resolve any conflicts encountered in their pursuit of adrenaline-fueled thrills. The bitterness Dustin harbored when Jake departed for an out-of-state college and later got married, thus ending their adventures, left such a profound impact on him that Dustin saw no point in cultivating new friendships. After all, what was the use of having a friend if they would inevitably leave you behind as they moved on to the next chapter of their life? Seeing no purpose in it, Dustin never bothered.

As he shifted into second gear, the caution signs along the canyon road whizzed past, warning drivers of the winding road. Dustin took it as a good omen when "Burnin' for You" started playing on the radio. Out of all the songs the DJ could've played, it had to be the one he had listened to on their last ride together. Dustin couldn't help but smirk. He had a good feeling about the drive.

She roared up the canyon road, the full moon hanging brightly in the partly cloudy sky. Its yellow light shined just the right amount of mystery over the dips and curves of Turnbull Canyon Road, making the drive an absolute thrill.

He missed the canyon road. To hell with Jake.

Dustin eased his foot off the clutch and shifted gears smoothly, with the power steering handling the sharp turns beautifully. His only hiccup was momentarily confusing the brakes with the clutch, which caused a brief transmission stall that he quickly corrected. From that point on, the ride was smooth...and fast.

Dustin was convinced. The 280ZX was officially his.

The following day, as expected, his beloved sister Lucy gave him an earful about the car, calling it frivolous. He told her to relax and chill out. Surprisingly, her boyfriend Richard was in awe of the new ride and even defended it.

"It's his money, Lucy. He can do what he wants with it," he said to her while admiring the car's polished frame outside the apartment complex they shared. Lucy tightened the strap on her blue bathrobe.

"How will you save money if you keep spending it like this?

Dustin grinned as he stuffed his hands into his jacket pockets.

Lucy shook her head. She didn't like Dustin's carefree attitude one bit. She composed herself with a deep breath because her irritation couldn't taint what she needed to say next. It took every ounce of her not to yell at her boneheaded brother.

"Dustin, the longer we stay here, the harder it'll be to save up. Because that's still the game plan, right? A house?"

"I haven't deviated from it, Lucy. Trust me, I want to move out of this dump as much as you do." It was valid, especially now with his new car. He didn't have a carport inside the gated apartment complex, so he wanted to avoid having her park outside by the main road without his close supervision.

"We'll get there, Lucy," Richard chimed in. "It will take some time, but we will."

Richard's brief words ended their argument. Still irritated about her brother's new car, Lucy went back inside to do her morning chores. Richard turned to Dustin and smiled light-heartedly, "Lovely car, Dustin."

"'Lovely' is a fag word to describe a car, Richard," Dustin interjected.

Richard winked at him. "Right." He headed toward their apartment unit on the first floor, near the laundry room that was always out of service. But then he turned around and asked, "Should I tell Lucy you'll be joining us for dinner?"

Dustin opened the driver's side door, placing his right foot inside the car and the other on the pavement. "I have plans."

Richard nodded and continued toward the security gate. He heard the heavy metal door of the car shut behind him.

The engine roared to life as Dustin turned the ignition.

Again, Richard stopped in his tracks. He couldn't help but turn around.

Dustin pulled away from the curb, executing a sharp U-turn in the opposite direction of the road, and bolted northbound, leaving Richard as a dwindling speck in his rearview mirror.

The countless reckless nights he had spent driving on highways, leaving many of his rivals in the dust, were one of the reasons Dustin rarely came home for dinner. It wasn't that he didn't like his sister's cooking; he loved it. But the road, its asphalt, paved more than just a way to get to places. To Dustin, it paved the way for adventure.

Street racing, house parties, and drive-in movies, where his favorite scenes were the bare-breasted women in his passenger-side seat, had become Dustin's life during the 1980s. These were his glory days, and they belonged to him.

What eventually ended those wild nights on the road wasn't his promise to his sister. Moving into their new home on Orr and Day Road was a high point in the rose-colored highlights of Dustin's prime. He didn't mind that the property was within earshot of the train tracks; after all, it was just a starter home, and it came at a reasonable price because of that.

The single-story house, supported by four white columns on the front porch, featured three bedrooms, two restrooms, a narrow kitchen, and a spacious living room. In a backyard that felt more like a ballpark, a towering tree stood dangerously close to a bedroom, its roots threatening the property's foundation. Much like a wisdom tooth, the tree needed to be cared for.

Despite the minor repairs required for the floors and walls, along with a fresh coat of paint inside and out, the house, with all its flaws, was theirs. If their estranged parents cared about their children, they would have been impressed at how their kids banded together to achieve a common goal despite their adversities.

Living in the house for a few years, life was almost perfect. Dustin wholeheartedly believed that his good times would never come to a screeching halt—a naive notion that later bit him in the ass. Dustin's life changed for the worse the day the troublemaker arrived.

~

"Dustin?" A voice called, jolting him awake from his memories into the present. Dustin wiped off the beads of sweat from his forehead. The shop's lack of ventilation was always a problem. Summers were unforgiving and merciless. But tonight, with the weather outside colder than the life he had built for himself, the dozen warm bodies that filled the building made it uncomfortably humid inside. It annoyed him. He turned toward the voice and saw Derek from the corner of his workstation. He was one of the few people Dustin tolerated at work.

"What do you want, Derek?" Dustin said.

Holding a Stella bottle in one hand, Derek approached him cautiously as if testing the waters of a shark-infested ocean. He replied, "What... what are you doing?"

"Thinking..."

Derek began working at the shop when he was the same age as Dustin, and like Dustin, he often complained about the management. When the company let him go during their reshuffling, he wasn't too concerned, as he had somewhat anticipated it. However, he found it troubling that the company callously let go of a veteran employee like Dustin.

Despite the challenges of working alongside him, Derek couldn't help but feel sorry for the guy.

"It's definitely a night for that," Derek replied. "Why don't you come and join the party?"

"They're junking my machine come Monday morning," Dustin grumbled. "How fuckin' stupid is that?"

Derek, uncertain of what to say, pressed his lips together and nodded.

Dustin turned away from him, retrieving his drink from the steel bed of his old NC. "This whole party is God damn stupid. It's a slap in the face!"

Light chatter filled the room while the band tuned their instruments for the next song, amplifying Dustin's belligerence.

Derek winced. He had approached Dustin intending to share a drink, but in retrospect, it might not have been the best idea. With a slight buzz from his three beers, Derek half-heartedly said, "It's not fair."

Those words ignited fury in Dustin's eyes, and Derek immediately regretted uttering them.

"You bet your fucking ass it's not fair!" Dustin retorted, bitterness lacing his words. He moved toward Derek, drink in hand. "If Walter's chubby offspring hadn't taken over the company, bulldozers wouldn't be lined up outside, ready to tear this place down to pieces!" In Dustin's view, Eddie's father could do no wrong, even capable of stopping the significant expansion of the Golden State Freeway that had forced the closure of all the stores along the strip of Firestone Boulevard.

Derek was on the verge of saying something to defuse the situation, but Edward, whom Dustin always considered the walking embodiment of a stubbed toe, emerged from the darkened corner of the workstation. He quickly demanded, through his pouty red lips, "Out. Out. Out. Dustin, I want you out."

"Like I give a damn about what you want," Dustin snapped back.

Mindful of his guests, Edward kept his voice in check and hastily added, "For Christ's sake, it's a Christmas party."

"Well, you've arranged it like a winter wonderland with enough snowflakes. Good job, Eddie. Great work," Dustin shot back. After years of hatred from working under Edward, they had reached a boiling point. Derek noted the tension between the two men, as coarse as the lines on their faces.

Edward didn't mince words either. Bluntly, he said, "You're a stubborn old drunk who refuses to learn anything new. You would have been gone long ago if you weren't part of my father's initial crew. You are as useless as that worn-down machine and just as antiquated. The only difference is that people would rather spend time with *it* than *you*. Now get the hell out of here before I call security."

Dustin straightened his posture, cocked his head up, and firmly added, "You don't have the guts."

Edward sighed. He was emotionally exhausted with him.

Suddenly, the lead singer's voice echoed through the microphone, announcing, "Alright, ladies and gentlemen. We'll slow it down with a Christmas classic you all probably know." The keys of a piano struck a melancholy tune. *"Christmas time is here,"* filled the room.

"Leave, Dustin. It's over. Move on with your miserable life," Edward said, his eyes filled with sorrow from the harsh truth. Turning to Derek, he added, "I'll see you out there, son."

Streaks of icy blue light pierced through the slight gaps and openings of the ancient NC machine, spilling onto the cold concrete floor near Dustin's feet.

Dustin and Derek, still in silence, watched Edward retreat into the party to salvage whatever holiday spirit remained in him. Meanwhile, the lead singer gently sang into the mic, leaving Derek and Dustin with a profound emptiness that left them feeling somber and lost.

~

"IIIPP!"

The blisters on his feet throbbed from another day of wandering the city, but what made him want to scream as he shuffled back home in December's damp chill wasn't the muscle pains coursing throughout his stiff legs. It was the need, the compulsion to utter a meaningless word.

"Iiippp!"

His spastic cry disrupted the sleepy, Christmas-decorated neighborhood. Yet, no one stirred in their warm beds. The residents knew his story and where he lived, so they slept tight through his empty cries.

"Iiippp!" Mist escaped Wally's breath and dissipated into the air. Parched from the cigarettes he loved to smoke and the sodas he liked to drink, Wally swallowed nothing as the itch—the tick, that uncontrollable part of his brain that made him strange—released him for the time being.

He spent the day the same way as any other day, loitering for change and bumming for cigarettes. Keeping a low profile after school hours was also part of his routine. The local teens had long ago figured out that by yelling "Ip" whenever they saw him hanging about the same strip malls as he did, he had no choice but to return with a louder, more substantial "Ip." Many of the kids and some of the adults dubbed him as "Ip."

The most recent incident of kids teasing him had occurred just a short time ago. Wally had collected enough change from his panhandling efforts to buy himself an orange soda and a bag of sour cream potato chips from the liquor store. He stood patiently in line, his mouth watering at the thought of quenching his thirst with a soda. Wally was always thirsty.

As he waited, a group of high schoolers walked into the store and immediately recognized him. Their giggles sent a shiver down Wally's spine. He wished he could run away, but that orange soda was calling his name.

The person ahead of him was taking an eternity, caught up in buying lottery scratchers from the cashier. Wally's anxiety mounted, and then, as he had dreaded, it finally happened.

"Iipp!" The shortest of the punk kids called out. The group erupted in laughter.

Wally's heart pounded, but he fought to keep his compulsion in check. He closed his eyes and pressed his lips tightly together. Beads of sweat formed on his forehead.

"Iip!"

Wally despised being different.

"Iip...Iip...li---"

"IIIIPPPP!" Wally cried out, startling both the cashier and the customer ahead. "Iiipp! Iiipp!" He couldn't control himself. It was like a fragile dam had finally given way, its torrential waters flooding the unsuspecting town below.

In his panic, he dropped his chips and soda. The soda can burst open, drenching his dirty, worn-out shoes in orange carbonated sugar.

"Iiipp!"

Wally bolted out of the liquor store, his shouts echoing down the street. Passersby gawked at the frantic figure.

It took Wally a whole hour to calm his mind. During that hour, he wandered the streets, yearning for a different life where he was known as Wallace, not the "IP man" of Norwalk. Wally couldn't remember the last time someone called him by his real name. Even his uncle didn't call him Wally. He had other, more cruel names reserved for him.

As he continued his walk home, he gripped his grimy hands around his faded green sweatshirt and sighed deeply. The memory of his uncle and the prospect of spending more time with him at home troubled Wally. It was one of the few coherent thoughts he was aware of, and it drove him to cry again, this time in anguish, "Iiiippp!"

The last house adorned with Christmas lights fell behind him. He stepped into the shadows that marked his approach to the darkest house near the railroad—his so-called "home." Except for the oil stains left behind from his uncle's old car, which he no longer had, the driveway was empty, signifying one thing: his uncle was out and about, getting intoxicated, growing angrier, and colder than the winter chill that swept through the city and forced Wally to retreat for the night.

Wally paid no attention to the front door. Instead, he lurched for the backyard. His well-worn white pair of sneakers carried him across the uneven dirt alongside the thick tree that had been neglected and left standing. He pushed open a wooden gate, its latch having broken off.

In the backyard, a quiet jungle of weeds and rusted car parts, the fence creaked open like an excavated tomb. He emerged from behind the gate, lost in a fractured sense of clarity that came and went. The gate door teetered on its splintered frame as he approached the kitchen porch. But before he could reach the concrete steps that led to the weathered, chipped door, Wally stopped by an uncovered crawl space beneath the bathroom window. Its grate had been set aside in a reserved patch for gardening that never came to be.

He got on his knees, mud immediately dampening his kneecaps. The entrance to the crawl space, a dark, cobweb-covered chamber that would unnerve even the bravest soul, stared at him ominously as if daring him to enter.

Like an unwanted cough itching at the back of one's throat, his tic crept forward toward his nicotine-coated tongue. He wished he had another cigarette to smoke. Smoking always made the compulsion vanish.

Wally cocked his head to the side and closed his eyes. Slowly, with intense concentration and trembling fists that rested on his thighs, he pushed it away.

His raccoon-like eyes opened.

The hiccup was gone.

His muscles loosened and relaxed. Wally looked ahead into the darkness, into the crawl space.

"What's the point of giving you a damn key if you're just gonna lose it?"

Wally winced as he recalled his uncle's callous words. He shivered. The air was growing colder. Wally got on all fours and wormed into a den where lesser beings dwelled and thrived.

The soil dug deep into his fingernails as he pulled himself toward the dank smell of mold infesting the floorboards. Seasonal humidity and leaky pipes nurtured the cancerous black fungus, which permeated the household as an odd potpourri.

"If I find a shattered window or a broken door, I'll bust your nose and smash your balls. Got it? Stupid."

Something with eight legs slithered over his right hand and crawled away. Wally looked ahead, his eyes desperately scanning the pitch darkness for an indentation in the soil that he knew--

He slipped downward, his forehead bumping against a ridge he had created as a teenager to mark the spot beneath his closet. Stiff and awkward, Wally maneuvered off the ridge until he sat cross-legged inside a roughly dug-up pit. His mind was slipping in and out of a daze that had nothing to do with him bumping his head. Before his parents were killed in a car accident, resulting in the state awarding his uncle sole custody of him, his mother had once told him the name of his condition. But like a fool, he had forgotten it. All he could recall was that it rhymed with the word "autumn." Autumn was what he believed he had.

Wally shook away his fleeting thoughts. Collected, he looked up. A barely visible light peeked through the opening in the floor that led to his bedroom closet—his entryway home. Like a baseball catcher, Wally got on one knee and placed the other foot on the ground. Then, arching his back to avoid hitting his head on the floorboards, he slid open the cover cleanly.

Wally sprang to his feet and hoisted himself into the barren closet with ease. Being tall and lean, his head knocked on a few wire hangers that clattered and swayed against each other but didn't fall.

"Your useless ass is keeping me up with all your fuckin' cryin'. Maybe spending the night in the closet will teach you how to shut your mouth."

"Iiiiippp!!!"

As Wally heard the echo of the closet door being slammed shut all those years ago, he dusted himself off and added another layer of dirt that already encompassed the closet floor. The night he discovered the passageway for the crawl space in the dark prison his uncle threw him in every other night was when Wally gained the keys to his freedom. As a teen, when he finally dared to venture underneath the house, it allowed him to return home when he pleased. It was the independence he longed for, even if it just meant hanging around donut shops and liquor stores asking people for their change. For Wallace Potts—Wally...IP, it was a big deal.

The closet door creaked open.

Wally stepped into the messy bedroom. His bed, with its mattress meant for a child, was placed in the corner near two windows draped in a thin maroon sheet. On the stained carpet, a timeworn Mickey Mouse blanket lay on the floor, where empty soda cans—mostly orange Sunkist—and personal classifieds ads of seductive half-naked women were scattered throughout the dated room. He was home, but nothing was comforting about being home.

Wally's thirst grew heavier. He needed something to drink or at least something to smoke. Standing on solid concrete all day, the carpet felt foreign as Wally made his way to the door, like stepping on a dry sponge.

In the living room, he emerged from the dark hall. Soft moonlight emanated through the partially drawn curtains, giving the cheap wood panel decor and all its dust-laden trappings a sense of isolation that made Wally uneasy. He tottered to the kitchen and noticed his uncle's seat across the way. The shabby green recliner and its reading stand remained cloaked in shadows despite being near a window.

Wally opened the fridge, squinting away from its bright light. With his eyes adjusted to it, he looked through the items inside, but there wasn't much. Slices of deli ham, bread, a block of cheddar cheese, and an open can of chili beans. No soda. No water. Only four cans of beer.

Wally took out a PBR and closed the fridge. He knew drinking any of his uncle's beers was prohibited, but tap water wouldn't cut it tonight.

As Wally entered the living room again, he popped open the can of beer and steadily drank it with both hands, thankful that none of it spilled on the floor.

Abruptly, the glare of his reflection coming off a glass display case caught his attention. It was his uncle's trophy cabinet, a monstrous three-shelf unit with a loose front right leg, teetering precariously and threatening to topple with the slightest nudge. In the 30 years the cabinet loosely stood, it never fell. Inside the cabinet, a jumble of knickknacks from city lake vacation spots, typewritten certificates, and age-stained photographs filled the locked shelves. Amidst the overflowing mementos, one object always stood out to Wally.

On the top shelf, nestled between a bowling trophy and a marble-green bowling ball from a victorious game in 1980, Wally's gaze always gravitated towards an 8 x 10 photograph of a bowling team. In between a bowling league, he saw his Mom and Dad side by side in their matching black and yellow uniforms. His Mom held one side of the trophy while his uncle had the other end. Both were gleaming with joy, which was a rare sight if anyone knew his uncle.

"You like that picture, huh? That was before you were born. Back when we were happy. You know? You're the reason they're dead."

"Iiipp!" Wally shouted, interrupting the quiet home. He was too young to remember the day of the car accident, but even as a child, he knew his uncle was right. His parents were dead because of him. If he hadn't been born with special needs, they would still be alive, living far away from his uncle's spiteful control.

Wally turned away from the picture frame and the cabinet in which it was encased. His lingering thoughts of what could've been exhausted him more than the walk back home. Sipping his beer, he hobbled his way to the green recliner. He sank into the seat. His knees spread apart awkwardly like skinny tree branches.

The TV remote was on a side table beside a stack of classic car magazines and a portable radio, but he had no interest in watching whatever was playing on the tube. Wally knew that his uncle would return soon; this time, it wouldn't be just for the night. His retirement meant they would have to spend more time together, a prospect that filled Wally with dread.

~

It was a clear spring Saturday night, and the clock struck 2 a.m. The air was crisp and refreshing. Young patrons filled the parking lot with boisterous chatter outside a hip local bar. Unbeknownst to the rowdy crowd of social smokers, faint headlights emerged from the west side of the four-lane road. The rumbling growl of a powerful engine soon followed it.

Behind the wheel of his cherished car, Dustin shifted gears with the windows rolled down. His glassy eyes blazed with drunken fury, and his shaggy gray hair whipped wildly. He had recently endured weeks of indoor confinement due to a heavy storm that had swept the West Coast. Waiting out the rain had been maddening, even in his spacious home. Day and night, his infuriating nephew's tics had become increasingly unbearable. He was on the verge of losing control and knocking him out, but Dustin found it more challenging to handle him as the brat grew older and taller. Wally was no longer a child. He had transformed into a vacant-eyed oddity Dustin had the misfortune of caring for. Of course, Dustin had attempted to go out one rainy night to drink, and on his way back home from the bar, he nearly ran over a kid on a skateboard. That close call had sobered him up until the rain subsided.

With the rain long gone, Dustin stumbled out of the Powwow Saloon, thoroughly wasted. In his town, the local bars knew him all too well, and consequently, none of the watering holes he frequented wanted anything to do with him. This pushed him to venture a bit farther than he would have preferred just to get a damn drink.

The last genuinely great bar in Norwalk, at least in his not-so-humble opinion, had been Bobo's. But Bobo's had vanished for good, like so many other things he cherished in his youth. Much to the relief of the community and local law enforcement, Bobo's had been demolished in the early 2000s, leaving old-school winos and troublemakers like him without a familiar haunt to get plastered in. A new generation, what Dustin derogatorily called "snowflakes," had taken over his town, and he detested them almost as much as the idiot he shared his home with.

However, that night at the Powwow Saloon, before his car became actual scrap metal, all his animosity toward the new was temporarily set aside with each drink and song.

Gin and tonic led to AC/DC.

Rum and coke took him to Tom Petty.

Whisky on the rocks came with a little splash of Supertramp.

And Pabst Blue Ribbon hammered him right into Led Zeppelin.

With the saloon's tavern-like decor, he was mentally transported back to 1979. Dustin felt reborn. The only thing missing was his old pal Walter, but the poor son of a bitch had died of a stroke during the tail end of the Reagan administration. This resulted in the apple of his eye, his son Eddie, taking over the shop and freezing Dustin's pay increases until he updated his skill set. He never did.

When the last call finally came at one-thirty-five, he was far from ready to call it quits. Instead, as people began to leave the bar, he slumped in the driver's seat of his car and contemplated an enticing idea that thrilled him.

Turnbull Canyon Road.

Dustin almost mumbled the words. He pushed the idea of a canyon drive away. It was too late for that kind of ride. But as he inserted the key into the ignition and turned it, the muffled speakers came to life. The unmistakable intro of his anthem, "I Drink Alone" by George Thorogood, began to play. The rebellious and fierce guitar and saxophone riffs rattled the metal interior of the car.

Dustin glanced at the rearview mirror, noticing that his eyes still looked young, even though the rest of his face suggested otherwise.

Fuck that. I ain't no old fart.

He reversed his car and awkwardly peeled out of the parking lot just as Thorogood declared that he liked to drink alone.

Speeding down Firestone Boulevard, he caught all the green lights. He shifted gears, and to his amazement, his car was driving like new. It was as if her transmission had never blown out when she was racing against one of those bullshit carbon fiber cars some years ago. It had taken him much time and effort to get her back up and running. Car parts for her had become scarce during the years before she was out of commission. Sure, the internet could have made it easier for him, but Dustin never bothered to learn how to use a modern computer. The Yellow Pages, that was his Google. His search engine. When he was scrambling to fix her, despite a thin tarp protecting her from the elements, the sun had battered her glossy coat into a spectacle that couldn't be polished away. When she was finally able to hit the road again, she wasn't the same. She drove sluggishly, and her guts stirred like a ship. Still, he was glad to have her back.

Barreling through the empty road, Dustin struggled to keep his vision straight.

"Come on, you fucking pussy," Dustin heard his younger self egging him on. "Don't tell me you're fucking tired." Suddenly, Dustin's twenty-six-year-old self appeared in the passenger seat, his hair and leather jacket vibrant.

"Screw you," Dustin mumbled, his muscles tightening as he pushed his bitchin' ride ahead.

"That's what I'm talking about, baby!"

The Datsun roared past the trendy bar, causing patrons to watch and gasp at its reckless speed.

The intersection rapidly approached, and the crucial left turn was coming up fast.

"You got this, baby! You got this!"

Dustin merged onto the left shoulder and lifted his foot from the gas pedal. Then, with fearless determination, he navigated the turn without slowing down, closing his eyes briefly as memories of his carefree youth rushed back. The engine's roar calmed in that fleeting moment, and the car became as silent as the early morning. A brisk gust of wind flowed through the open windows, refreshing his flushed cheeks and filling his lungs with cold air.

"Yeah, baby! Yeah!"

He felt the weight of the car shift to the left. Then...

Dustin's beloved ride, faithfully by his side for three decades, careened uncontrollably into a pawn shop at the intersection of San Antonio Drive and Firestone Boulevard. The reinforced double-glass doors, protected by sturdy bars, proved futile in halting the relentless force of his wild driving. Fragments of shattered glass and splinters of various guitars and assorted items erupted in a chaotic explosion before the broken windshield. Despite the wisdom of wearing his seat-belt that fateful night, it couldn't prevent Dustin's head from colliding with the steering wheel, rendering him unconscious as his vehicle finally ground to a halt in the wrecked pawn shop. The mangled hood spewed crumpled black rubber hoses and twisted steel while the radiator hissed like a disgruntled heckler at a comedy club.

A few minutes later, he gradually regained consciousness, his mind shrouded in a dreamy haze. A concerned crowd had gathered around the scene.

He caught fragments of their conversations, but his attention waned as the distant sirens drew nearer. He awoke once more to what sounded like a tin can being pried open—it was his car door. With a bloody face and a swelling black eye, Dustin looked up and saw a towering figure standing over him. The stranger's face remained hidden behind the glare of a powerful flashlight. The only detail Dustin could make out was the sheriff's badge, its edges gleaming like a distant star.

"You're going to be okay," Dustin heard the figure say.

To which Dustin replied, "My car..."

He did not respond, but Dustin knew she was marred beyond restoration. Even if he could miraculously resurrect her once more, his towering medical bills, the fees incurred from his DUI charge, and the costs to repair the shattered pawn shop had rendered him financially incapable of reviving her. The only car he could now afford was a '94 Corolla, cou-pled with the court-mandated breathalyzer he needed to install to start his "new" lame ride — which refused to turn on the night he was thrown out of the Christmas party.

The breathalyzer test beeped excessively.

Frustrated, Dustin pounded his fists on the steering wheel.

"Fuck!" In his right hand, he clenched a long hose under-neath the dashboard. The constant beeping abruptly ceased.

After he caught his breath, Dustin blew into the apparatus, only to receive the same exasperated response.

"Goddamnit..."

A gray pickup truck pulled up behind him and honked. Dustin glanced over his shoulder awkwardly and saw Derek's Toyota Tacoma through the dewy window.

Derek rolled down the window, unaware of the real cause of Dustin's car trouble. He hollered, "Do you need a jump?"

Dustin came out of the car and approached Derek. The noise from the 5 freeway, separated by a flimsy fence, had him hollering, too. "No. I need a ride." Another intoxicated incident could attract the authorities, and Dustin was fortunate that Derek was a good kid.

"Sure, hop in."

He went to the passenger seat of Derek's pick-up truck without bothering to lock his car.

"Take me to Front Street. Do you know where that is?"

"Yes, sir."

As Derek pulled from the parking lot, Dustin couldn't help but steal one final, melancholy gaze at the old machine shop. He saw the demolition excavator quietly stationed in a shadowy corner. As Derek turned left, the machine shop slowly faded from Dustin's view, leaving a profound sense of loss and nostalgia tugging at his bitter heart.

~

Dustin's alcohol-laced breath carried his usual stories, the same ones Derek had heard countless times before. He passionately and vulgarly lamented how music "just wasn't the same anymore," not like back in his day when "music kicked ass." Up until Dustin launched into a racist rant that filled the rest of the drive to Front Street, Derek had tolerated Dustin's repetitive stories. It reminded Derek of his grandfather, who told him the same old stories but never aired grievances about the changing city due to the "Spanish" moving in.

"That's what happens when liberals take over the government, Derek. We get a state bombarded by wetbacks and their damn anchor babies. We put 'em all on buses and drive their taco-asses back to Mexico. Hell, I'll do it myself if they asked me to." Dustin leaned forward as he spotted his destination. "Well, son, this is my stop."

Derek heaved a sigh of relief. He pulled over to the side of an empty street. It was miles away from any residential area, surrounded only by shuttered industrial shops that gave the place a desolate, ghost-town feel.

Turning to Dustin, Derek furrowed his brow. "Where are you off to?"

"I'm going to grab a drink at the American Legion. Want to join me?" Dustin replied.

Derek glanced to his left, spotting a discreet blue and red neon sign on the side of a beige building. It read: American Legion Post 359.

He chuckled awkwardly. "Nah, I'm done for the night." He turned to Dustin just as he opened the car door. A rush of cold air greeted him, prompting Derek to bundle up in his Dickies jacket.

"It was good knowing you, Derek," Dustin said, extending his hand.

Derek accepted the gesture and shook hands firmly. "Likewise."

"Don't ever change," Dustin advised.

Derek managed a forced smile, his parting words carrying a hint of unease. "Good luck, Dustin."

Dustin stepped outside and closed the passenger door. As the pickup truck's taillights faded into the distance, he headed toward the American Legion. He grasped the metal handle as he reached the door, illuminated by a solitary light. However, the heavy red door refused to budge.

Dustin muttered. He tugged on the handle again, but it remained firmly shut.

"Hey!" he pounded his palm against the door. "It's too early to be closed!" He was right. The Legion staff was out on Christmas vacation. His frantic pounding continued until his palm felt hot and raw. Eventually, he gave up, defeated.

Dustin resisted the urge to sigh, considering it a sign of weakness. He weighed his options; another bar was a block away on Firestone Boulevard. But he dreaded being recognized as the guy who had crashed into the pawn shop several months ago. He didn't want that kind of attention.

Instead, he turned on his heel and walked away, shoving his hands into the pockets of his worn leather jacket. He felt the seams of the pockets stretched and rip. He had no choice but to head back home, the burden of his bleak future pressing heavily on his shoulders.

~

His shoes shuffled through the white gravel. The train tracks offered the best chance of avoiding the watchful gaze of the LA County Sheriffs.

As a boy, Coast Grain was vital to the city's economy. As he walked along the railway to school, he could still recall the aroma of fresh grains filling the air along the boulevard. However, those operations had ceased, creating a large shopping center that many of the city's residents relied on. The air was thick these days, and there was a smell of motor oil and urine in the railroad, courtesy of the modern age.

The walk was long and clumsy due to the loose gravel. Graffiti-covered walls gave way to a small park enclosed by a fence. Beyond the park, he entered an open field where the tracks split into two directions. In the distance, a homeless encampment was also coming into view. He veered to the right, following the steel tracks that led him toward their makeshift community.

A few homeless individuals sought warmth by a makeshift bonfire flickering inside a metal trash can. Despite their peculiar and ragged appearances, Dustin felt no fear. He had grown weary of living. As much as he wished for one of them to end his suffering, none of the city's forgotten souls paid him any mind as he trudged home.

The train tracks beside his feet led to a concrete tunnel. Dustin entered it, and the darkness enveloped him like a black hole.

A shadowy figure emerged from the darkness on the other end of the tunnel. It was Dustin. He completed the remainder of the journey without incident, with only his thoughts as the relentless monsters haunting his path home.

What am I going to do with myself?

He sighed, and his misty breath billowed out.

I need a drink.

Shivering, Dustin approached Orr and Day Road. He had finally made it home.

I hope that shit is in his room.

In the fridge, a few beers awaited him. They were the only thing he was looking forward to. Dustin made a right at the railroad crossing. Emerging from the wild bushes that shielded the railroad from oncoming traffic, his house came into view.

It looked abandoned due to its lack of care. Cutting through the dry lawn, he slouched up the porch steps, which stretched and creaked beneath his feet.

Inside the musty house, the front door swung open. Dustin reached for the light switch by the doorway. A pair of dim reading lamps near the door flickered on. As he closed the door and headed for the kitchen, he failed to notice his nephew seated in his favorite chair. Dustin was too focused on getting something to drink to see anything else. His sole objective was to obtain a can of beer. He opened the fridge, only to find his drinks were gone.

"Son of a bitch!" Enraged, he slammed the fridge shut. "I'm gonna kill that—"

Suddenly, the radio turned on. A boisterous voice blared from the speakers, jarring Dustin to a halt.

"I gotta tell you, Johnny, life has nothing on fiction. But whatever happened in Roswell, we'll never know," the radio guest said.

Dustin spun around to see his nephew casually sipping his beer as if he were taunting him.

Decker's laughter rattled the speaker. "No, I guess we won't, and that's what makes it interesting."

Dustin stomped his way over to Wally, his muscles tightening with anger. "Jesus Christ, boy. You smoke all my smokes, and now you drink all my beer?" Dustin marveled at the three empty cans on the reading table.

Wally glared at him and defiantly took another swig of his uncle's beer. The radio host was bidding farewell to his guest as Dustin angrily demanded, "Get off my seat!"

"Ip!" Wally shot back.

"Get off my goddamn seat!"

"Iiiipp!!!"

"Alright, folks. 'The Breakup Song' by the Greg Kihn Band will carry us into the break. We'll be back right after this."

"If you don't get off my seat, Lord help me, I'll—"

"Iiiii--!!!" Dustin slapped him hard, knocking the beer can flying from his hand.

Wally slowly straightened himself, a scowl washed over his face. His eyes filled with tears as he spoke through a trembling lip, "I hate you."

It was the first time Dustin had ever heard his nephew say something coherent, and the gravity of Wally's words left him stunned. As the shock wore off, his silence quickly turned to rage. He raised his hand, ready to strike Wally again.

"You stupid son of—"

Wally launched himself from the chair with a thunderous roar, propelling Dustin backward until he collided with the wall. The impact sent a pair of delicate picture frames crashing to the ground.

Both men grappled with the ferocity of unsupervised children in a playground fight. Fists swung through the air, rib bones were bruised, and hair was yanked. Dustin grabbed his nephew by the shirt and threw him against the trophy cabinet. The impact sent the cabinet's contents crashing to the bottom of the shelves and jostled the already loose leg even more.

Fueled by rage, Wally overpowered him and slammed Dustin against the same cabinet. The glass doors shattered under the force. Wally repeatedly slammed his uncle into the cabinet, obliterating the precious memories held inside.

"Iiipp...Iiipp...IIIPPP!!!"

Dustin planted his feet firmly and, mustering a burst of strength, repelled his nephew's relentless assault. He shoved Wally away and tackled him forcefully to the floor, causing the loose front leg of the cabinet to wobble loose. Its leg finally fell off. As the cabinet swayed precariously, Wally and Dustin continued their fight on the floor beneath it. Like a weakened tree long overdue to fall, the cabinet finally gave way. The trinkets inside fell on them. The heaviest item—the marble-green bowling ball—tumbled from the top shelf and struck the back of Dustin's head with a loud thud.

Dustin's glasses shattered on the floor as his face slammed into the ground. Blood flowed freely from the back of his head, pooling on the floor as the bowling ball rolled away. With the cabinet toppled and its contents strewn about, a heavy silence surrounded the house, interrupted only by the radio show transitioning into its scheduled commercial break.

****

In the sterile confines of a secure medical facility, where the boundaries of day and night seemed to dissolve into a haze, a female nurse with her hair neatly pinned back moved with practiced precision. The fluorescent lights cast a constant, unchanging glow, creating a sense of timelessness as she glided down the hallway, her footsteps echoing softly. Each measured step was part of a rhythm that seemed to have no beginning or end, as if time itself had become an indistinct, endless loop, blurring the lines between hours, days, and weeks.

She checked each room in turn, peering through the small window portals and meticulously recording her observations on her clipboard. As she proceeded to the next room, she slid open the portal.

A soft voice emerged from the shadows within. "Can I have a cigarette, please?" the patient pleaded.

The nurse responded sternly, "I told you before. There is no smoking."

"Okay," he meekly responded.

Inside the holding room, the window portal closed. Wally, dressed in gray sweats, shuffled toward the undersized bed. He lowered himself onto the plastic mattress and curled into the corner, drawing his knees close to his chest.

Outside the room, as the nurse went about her rounds, Wally's cries reverberated down the empty hallway. "Iipp...Iipp...Iiipp!"

Sponsored Break

Johnny Decker took a sip from his favorite mug, listening to the fading jingle of an insurance commercial through his headphones. Janet's familiar hand signal told him it was time to start the show.

"I have to admit, folks, I like that little jingle—*'Rest assured at Rest Insurance.'* Yeah, I know, I'm a bit weird," Decker chuckled. "All right, we've got open phone lines coming up. So, grab your cell phone or even that old landline and tell us your weirdest, most outrageous stories. But there is a catch. They have to be real."

Johnny's excitement was palpable. "It's going to be a blast, folks. Hang tight; we'll be right back after this brief message."

The sound of ocean waves crashing against a rugged cliff marked the end of the show's final break, following a brief silence.

Contact the author: delsalvobooks@gmail.com

Follow my journey on social media:
Facebook: The Late Hour, Stories for the Insomniac